The Theft of The Huntsman

Master Thief Series, Volume 1

S.K. O'Brien

Published by Sammantha Saffell, 2024.

THE THEFT OF THE HUNTSMAN

First edition. August 19, 2024.

Copyright © 2024 S.K. O'Brien.

ISBN: 979-8227754134

Written by S.K. O'Brien.

Also by S.K. O'Brien

Master Thief Series
The Theft of The Huntsman

Ride Or Die Series
The Queens

The Daemon Brothers
Anguish

Chapter One

It was a humid summer night with the sound of rolling thunder just in the distance. Flashes of lighting lit up the clouds. The warm wind was picking up. A storm was building in the distance. It would fill the sky sooner rather than later. Rain would fall for at most fifteen minutes, cooling us all for twenty minutes and then the humidity would return. Savannah, Georgia was a beautiful city filled with history, ghosts of its past, and a small town feel. It was also hot and humid, making me wish I was somewhere else on a different job, somewhere that was less humid. The problem is that this job was too damn important for me to walk away from. I was here for one reason and one reason only, a painting called Love and Dread by Edvard Munch. He was the artist that was best known for The Scream. For me, The Scream was an intriguing painting but I had always felt that Love and Dread was a more moving painting. It was a beautiful depiction of what love was meant to be, one that moved my soul. Some felt the painting was of a woman kissing the neck of her lover as he rested his head in her lap. Others believed she was a vampire draining her lover. I knew the painting well and it was none of those things. The painting was about a female showing love to her lover as he wept. The brush strokes were rough giving the painting that slight textured look. Each stroke showed through the few colors that were used within the image.

I knew everything about the painting. It had been created in the late eighteen-hundreds at the beginning of his career. Edvard made three copies: one was in a museum in Sweden, one was in the home I was currently scouting, and the third had not been seen since its creation, or that was what the general population believed. I already had the third painting and had for the last ten years. It was one of my first heists I had ever pulled off successfully. As soon as I had it I knew what I needed to do. I needed all three paintings for my own collection. I wanted to be the beholder of such beauty. For most, I'm sure it sounds ridiculous, maybe even greedy, but it was not greed that drove me to do what I did, it was love, true love and admiration.

As I am sure you have put together, I'm an art thief or that is what society calls me. I see myself as a collector. I don't steal for the money. I steal for the thrill and for the love of art. The pieces I choose to acquire are pieces that move me in some way. From time to time, I steal small pieces that I can sell on the black market to keep my cash flow in the positive. The bigger pieces were for me. With that said, I only steal from private collections. Homes that could afford the loss and had terrible security for their art collection.

Tonight was a night of seeing what I was up against in terms of security. The man, Henry Augustus, owned the mansion and was a millionaire who liked to showcase his wealth any chance he got. Henry Augustus' family had been in Savannah for several generations, making money off of everything the south had to provide. The family was one of the oldest families in the city. Of the current surviving Augustus' family, Henry was the one running all of the business. He drank and smoked heavily as he flashed his money at every chance he could. From parties, getaway weekends, and even all four of his weddings. Henry Augustus was a man of money and power in Savannah. The problem with people like him, they felt they were invincible which meant security was the last thing on his mind. It almost made my job tonight even more enjoyable. I had spent a lot of hours studying not only the house but also the Augustus Family and like any other family, his family was a mess.

Henry Augustus had a teenage son from his first marriage. The son, Ethan, had been known to be a party boy. He had been arrested for driving under the influence several times, he had assault charges, and was an all-around rich brat. Henry and Ethan were alike in many ways and yet it was well known in the community that they hated one another.

The event tonight was like so many others he threw, a masquerade ball. I loved masquerade balls. They were a way for the rich to show off all that they had and made it easy for me to hide among the guests as I worked. The only downside with the theme was the heat of the night. I had picked out the lightest dress I could find, one that was stunning but also breathed. I was in a little black dress with no sleeves that hugged the upper half of my body. The bottom of the dress had an A-line that hit me mid-thigh. My dark auburn hair was pulled back into a bun on the back of my head, ensuring that my hair was out of my face. My mask was red with lace and sequins. To the right side of the mask were black and red feathers that covered the side of my head from the top to the base of my face. The mask was beautiful and ensured only my grey eyes showed and a quarter of my face. To complete the look, I added a red cape that flowed to my calf. I was in red pumps that had black lace over the red.

I walked around the edge of the party as people talked with one another. Drinks were flowing freely, which ensured most of the party goers were already tipsy within the first hour. With any luck, no one would remember seeing me. I scanned the outdoor party finding each of the exits. There were a total of three, two on each side of the house and one at the far back side of the large property.

The back of the house had a long set of stairs that went from the house to the grassy area that was green and perfectly manicured. The stairs were narrow at the top and became wider as it moved downward. At the base of the stairs it became a circular patio. The owners of the house started the party with a grand entrance with his new trophy wife who was twenty years younger than he was. It was his favorite way to get the attention he craved.

The outside of the house had sections that protruded out, creating spaces that provided nooks for two or three balconies. The windows were long and thin with several panes of glass. In between every two or three windows were windows in the shape of archways. The amount of windows for the entire house was a security risk. Most of the windows did not open so they probably had no sensor on them. With the right skills, anyone could enter into the house unnoticed.

Off the main house was a round pool with a waterfall that poured directly from the pool down to a small fountain that was lit with blue lights. Around the pool was a lounge area that was decorated with white string lights. A pool house sat to the right of the house. The pool house was really just a smaller version of the house.

Placed in between the main house and the pool house was a gazebo. Inside of it was more patio furniture. The place had probably six different areas where they could sit and lounge.

Next up was studying the security team. The four guards on duty looked like amateurs. They had placed themselves at two of the exits, missing one exit entirely. Two out of the four were out of shape and had one too many donuts which meant I could easily outrun them if needed. The other two seemed to be in better shape which probably meant they could catch me, but I had potions within my purse that would slow them down. There was a good chance that on a normal day there would be only two guards at most. I was betting the owner of the property didn't believe in keeping guards on the property at all times. I watched the security team as they chatted with one another, not paying much attention to what was happening around them. These were guards that didn't really care what they were protecting; they just wanted the paycheck. They would be less likely to take a chance to stop me.

The big issue was going to be navigating the house. It was a tudor style house but on a much larger scale. The house was wide and spacious with several rooms and floors. The two main floors with fifteen rooms, five bathrooms, two living rooms, and a basement that stretched the length of the house. The basement was broken into two rooms, or that was according to the floor plans I had found. One room was for his art collection of eight different paintings on full display. The other room was for the security system. I had studied the plans for hours, memorizing every inch of the mansion. The space in the basement was different from the rest. It was off. I suspected that the basement had a third room but I wouldn't know until I gained access to the room.

I had already begun to check out the security system outside of the guards. There were small round cameras that were placed every ten to twelve feet along the perimeter of the house. I knew the camera system. They were small cameras that could pick up movement about thirty feet out from where the camera was positioned. It meant close to the house was monitored more than the grassy area or the surrounding woods.

I had already walked through a number of rooms within the house. Henry painted the rooms in many shades of white. There were plush sofas in several rooms that appeared to be hardly used. Inside the house there were no cameras in any of the rooms, making it easier to move through the house. I was betting that there was a security system for the basement similar to the one outside. I had two options for the security system: I could use a laser to disable the cameras which would force me to move quickly and less neatly. It would ensure I made a mistake. I would have to deal with any security that would be watching the cameras as they came to investigate why the cameras failed.

My second option was to find a way into the computer system and shut it down. It would buy me more time as the team would reset the system. It would take several minutes for the system to come up. By then, I would have the painting and would be gone. There was always the chance that I would hit a firewall I couldn't get through or a second server off site. I was leaning towards the second option but there were a variety of issues that could arise.

Eventually, I moved through the party speaking to several of the party goers, making small talk as I moved. There were probably at least three hundred people here. As the party continued more people continued to arrive. I headed to the bar, wanting a glass of wine.

"What can I get you?" The man behind the bar asked.

"White wine." I spoke.

"We only have Sauvito Sauvignon. Are you okay with that?"

"That's fine." I smiled softly.

The man poured me a glass of wine and handed it to me. I turned to face the party and took a sip of the wine. It was a sweet wine with a small taste of lemon on the end. I looked at the party goers as they drank and talked with one another. Stealing the painting tonight would be my best opportunity. Most of the party goers were already heading toward being drunk so they would not remember my presence. I was beginning to think through my next move when a male approached the bar. He was dressed in a basic tuxedo but one that fit perfectly, telling me that it was a tailored suit.

"Can I get a Bourbon?" He asked the bartender.

"Would you like to hear our options of brands?"

"No. Just pour whatever you have." I gave the male a side glance as I sipped my wine. "You seem to be out of place just as I am." The male spoke to me.

"What makes you say that?" I asked.

"You have spent most of your time alone only speaking to a few people here and there, never for more than a few minutes, which tells me that you are only engaging in small talk. You spend more time on your own than you do with any one individual."

I looked at the male, impressed but also suspicious of how much he had been watching me.

"Interesting theory."

"Theory?" He raised an eyebrow at me.

"Yes, theory."

The male looked at me, giving me a smile making his green eyes light up.

"Are you telling me you enjoy parties like this?"

"You didn't say I enjoyed them, you said I wasn't comfortable." I pointed out.

"Comfort and enjoyment generally go hand in hand."

"Not always." I smiled at him.

He took a drink of his bourbon and moved away from the bar. I couldn't help but follow him.

"In that case, you are comfortable but not having fun."

"I would agree with that. What about you? What makes this event uncomfortable for you?" I asked.

"I get bored with superficial people."

I smiled at his answer. I knew how to blend in with people.

"I can understand that. This is not what I would call exciting or fun."

"It makes me think of high school."

I laughed at the description.

"Because of all the cliques and how they pretend to like one another when in reality they can't stand one another."

"Yes! I expect them to tell me I'm not cool enough to sit with them."

I laughed at him harder. His green eyes were sharp as he gave me a smile. He was a hellborn just like I was. The difference was he was a wolf and I was a witch. Everyone else here was human, including the security guards.

The male was handsome. He had a chiseled jaw with some rough stubble that ran along his jawline. The mask he was wearing was black with copper sun in the center of the forehead and thick design of fleur de lis in a roman style. It had satin straps that tied on the back of his head. He had broad shoulders with thick arms and a narrow waist. I would say he was around five ten as he stood next to me.

"Jasper Wolf."

He held out a hand to me. I shook his hand.

"Kathrine Cascade." I lied.

As a thief, I had several identities I used for events such as this one. For this party, I was Kathrine Cascade, a female who owned a wine company. It was an identity I had not used in several years but one I still knew well and kept alive.

In the art theft world and the black market, I was known as Red. No one knew my real name, at least not anyone alive did. My true name was Phoenix Redmont and I was more than an art thief. I was also an earth witch who used my abilities to help me flourish as a thief. I had potions for knocking individuals' unconscious. I had a few that could alter my scent enough to hide it.

"Nice to meet you." Jasper gave me a subtle look as he checked me out. I smiled at him, knowing he was enjoying the view as much as I was enjoying looking at him.

"So, if you don't enjoy events like this, what are you doing here?"

"I own a business and whether I like it or not, I need people like this. Coming to these events allows me to mingle and develop relationships with people who can help my business grow." I lied. "How about you?"

"I'm here for work as well."

I raised an eyebrow.

"What kind of work do you do?"

"I work for an insurance company called Icarus." Jasper explained.

I kept the smile on my face even though I wanted to panic. Icarus was one of the biggest insurance companies that had been growing in recent months to expand their investigation department. They had the largest, most comprehensive database regarding art thieves and pieces that have been stolen over the last ten years. Icarus had even gone as far as working on a new security system that they could provide their clients with for an extra fee. The company was a pain in my ass and of all the males I could have talked to he was part of it. I needed to get out of here.

"Jasper!" A man who was tall and thin approached us. "Have you seen this security staff? They're a joke. These guys can't even do a proper perimeter check let alone stop a thief." The man seemed odd, almost a little too outraged about the choices the owner of the house had made.

"Silas, there is nothing we can do about the security team he chose. He was given parameters that he was required to meet and he did."

"The hell we can't. If any of his pieces go missing, we're not approving any payouts."

I could see the frustration in Jasper's face at his associate. His smile became tight and the fun he and I were having a moment before slipped away.

"According to the policy, he needs to have a security team of at least four people who are armed when he is having an event. He has that. He is required to have a security system that has cameras and he did that. If, by chance, someone makes a move to steal something, he has done his part as the owner. As the representatives of Icarus, we will do our part and investigate." Jasper explained to his colleague.

"Come on Jasper, you and I both know he found the cheapest security he could find."

"If that is the case it will be in my report."

"When it happens because you and I both know it will, you better do your job. If you do a payout for this asshole I will let the company know you fucked up. I will not allow my name to be tied to this mess."

Silas was an A-one asshole who I was growing to dislike greatly. He was closer to six feet tall and built thin. When I say thin, I mean he was maybe a hundred and sixty pounds soaking wet. The human had dark brown eyes and hair. His hair was kept shaved close to the scalp but you could see he was starting to go bald with a deep widow's peak where Jasper had a sharp jawline and was handsome. Silas was plain looking in his all black suit. Maybe if he wasn't standing next to Jasper he would be handsome but I doubt it.

"I have been doing this for a long time, Silas. I know what I'm doing."

"Do you?"

"Yes, I do Silas. As the senior investigator, you will follow my lead." Jasper voice held a new edge to it.

"This is bullshit!"

"This is business. His policy requires he meets certain provisions and he has."

"Cheap bastard."

I took another sip of my wine as I stood there listening to the two of them argue. Jasper said nothing for a moment. I watched as he tried to steady himself before he spoke again.

"Silas, this is part of being an investigator. We ensure our clients are meeting their policy requirements and if something goes wrong, it's our responsibility to attempt to retrieve the property." Jasper said.

"Our policies need to be written stronger, forcing our clients to take thefts more seriously." Silas complained.

"Until that happens, we do the best we can do. Now, have a drink and enjoy the rest of your evening."

"How do you stay so damn calm?"

Jasper smiled at Silas.

"Because I'm the best at what I do and I do not worry about the small things."

Silas gave him a look that I couldn't quite decipher.

"Will I ever know all of your tricks?" Silas asked.

"You know the answer to that."

Silas ordered a gin tonic as we stood there. He took a drink as soon as the glass was handed to him.

"As your partner, don't you think I should be as good as you, Jasper?" I could hear the jealousy in his voice.

Jasper took a drink of his bourbon.

"I think you should be as good as you can be, which doesn't equate to you being as good as me." Jasper smiled as he swirled his glass slowly.

Silas shook his head. The look made it clear he hated Jasper.

"I'm going to go make the rounds."

Silas walked away from us as he pushed through the crowd.

"Sorry about my colleague." Jasper turned his attention back to me.

"It's not a problem, people get passionate about what they do. So, you're an investigator for an insurance company?"

Jasper smiled at me.

"I am and when Silas isn't passionate about protecting art, he wants to beat me."

"To beat you?" I questioned.

"Yes."

"Are you that good?"

"I'm the best Icarus has."

I wanted to ask him how that was possible. Icarus was a company that only hired humans. Of course, the company always said that they were an equal opportunity company but as a hellborn we all knew that wasn't true. They operated like any law enforcement branches did. Hellborns were not to be trusted. We were the monsters and the humans needed to be protected from us. It was a belief that I was unsure would ever change.

I wanted to ask Jasper how he was able to land a job as an investigator. Instead, I began to work on my exit strategy from the situation and the party. I knew there was an exit to the right and left of the house and there was another on the back of the property. The exits on the sides of the house would have caught my face on the camera. I had the mask on but I didn't want the security system to have too many images of me. The right software could piece together my image. The back of the property would be the best exit but it would look odd if I exited from the back of the property. There were enough people here that I could get lost in the crowd but not necessarily, not with this male. He would be watching my every move.

"Is it always like this with him.?" I continued the conversation.

"He usually hides it better than he is tonight but yes."

"You don't sound like you like him."

Jasper took a drink and gave me a look.

"I wouldn't say I dislike him."

"He's a pain in the ass, isn't he?" I asked.

Jasper laughed.

"That's an understatement. He's like the straight A student who has to be better than everyone else in the room and yet he never is better."

"What's the problem with wanting to be the best?"

"With Silas, it's not being the best because you want to be good at what you do. It has more to do with him wanting to be seen as special." Jasper shook his head.

"Which means he isn't special at all." I added.

"Why do you say that?"

"Because, if he was special he wouldn't have any desire to show off. People that are special who have natural talent do not have the need for approval. They know they are."

"Agreed." Jasper's eyes linger at me before he looked around the party.

It was time to make my exit. I would have to use one of the side exits. I would pull my hood over my head and keep my face pointed towards the ground.

"Well, I should..."

"What are you doing tomorrow?" Jasper asked me before I could finish speaking.

His question caught me off guard.

"I am flying out tomorrow."

"Where to?"

"California." I lied.

"When will you be back in Georgia?"

I looked at Jasper. He was an attractive male and if he didn't work for Icarus I would have taken him up on his offer.

"I'm not exactly sure when. My business takes me all over the globe."

He reached into his breast pocket and handed me his business card. It was a thick white card that had his name written in bold letters across the center. Under his name was his number in smaller font.

"I will call you." I placed the card into my small clutch purse.

"Good. Until then, we have tonight."

Jasper smiled at me which made me want to stay and get to know him.

"I thought you were here working?" I asked.

"I am."

"How are you able to spend time with me if you are working?"

"My job was to ensure Mr. Augustus is meeting the requirements of the policy. I have done that and now I get to enjoy my drink and conversation with you."

I smiled at him. He had charm.

"It's that simple?"

"Tonight, yes it is. If I'm investigating a theft, not so much."

I wanted to know more.

"I would think it could get quite complicated for you." I replied.

"It can be. It depends on who I am looking for. For instance, the man who I believe is after a certain painting likes to pose as a staff member. I know he is a man who is around my height and is thin. He steals for money. There is another individual I am uncertain who they are or their tactics. I know they are good and that I have never found any of their pieces on the black market, which makes it difficult for me to find them or the art. I also am unsure why they steal."

"Is that important?" I asked.

"What?"

"Why they steal?" I asked.

"It gives me an idea of where to look. If I can't find the pieces on the black market, what are they stealing? Is it for the thrill?"

"Maybe it's both." I answered.

I didn't actually intend to respond to his thought process but I had become intrigued with the conversation and slipped up. I was cursing myself in my head when Jasper looked at me. It was a look that passed too quickly for me to decipher.

"People aren't that complicated."

"Some are." I retorted.

"Why do you say that?"

"Some people do things for more than one reason. Sometimes they make the choice because of how they were raised or because they believe what they are doing is right. Others like Silas do what they do because they want fame and fortune."

"Art thieves are different. They like the money."

"Are you sure about that?" I challenged him.

"I have been doing this for a long time, Katherine."

"I believe some would do it for money, but not all. Some, I would guess, like the thrill of stealing. Others may enjoy the art itself. Then you could have a fourth option which would be a combination more than one of those options."

Jasper's eyes narrowed at my answer.

"You seem to understand how individuals work."

"I have to in order to do what I do." I answered.

Jasper looked at me with a mixture of curiosity and suspicion. I had said too much. I had become wrapped up in the conversation instead of leaving when I should have.

"You said you owned your own business? What kind of business?"

"Wine."

"Wine?" Jasper answered.

I could see he was tasting the air around me. I was a master at lying, which meant it would be difficult for him to sense my lie but not impossible.

"Yes. I sell wine from several vendors and ensure new vendors have the opportunity to get their name out there for events like this."

Jasper looked at me, unsure if I was being honest. Before he could say anything an alarm began to sound from the house. A server from the party stood at the top of the long staircase, his body swaying slightly. I could see blood running down the side of his face.

"HELP ME!! PLEASE!" The server yelled.

There was a collective gasp and I watched as Jasper moved away from me and up the stairs. Silas was about three steps behind him. I gave the wolf one final look before I headed for the exit at the back of the property. I didn't look back as I moved. I stopped for only a second to remove my heels and continued to the exit. Of all the opportunities I had to steal the painting, I met a male who hunts art thieves. All the while, another illegal act was being committed.

Chapter Two

It took me an extra fifteen minutes to make it to my car. I drove away from the house as calmly as I could with my adrenaline pumping. The first rule of being a thief is when leaving a job you follow the law. Speeding, cutting through traffic, and driving aggressively is the fastest way to be caught.

My brain began to work overtime as I processed what I witnessed. The server could have been attacked by a drunk guest. It didn't seem like a viable option because no one within the house made an assault known. There was always the chance of a party crasher or someone who hated the Augustus family. They had made plenty of enemies over the years. I didn't believe that was the case. It could have been an attempted theft which seemed the most likely of the options. It could be someone who wanted random items within the house. Another possibility was someone was just casing the place, planning how to get in and out. Yet another possibility, as I knew all too well, it could very well be an art thief like me.

I drove home, checking my mirrors regularly as I drove out of the city. No car followed me as I hit the city limit. I had a small cabin set up outside of Savannah, Georgia, in the middle of the woods. Most of the properties in this area were only used during certain times a year. All of them were spread out over several acres. The tree in this particular forest grew tall and wide creating almost a tunnel of trees around the dirt roads around here. There were hills of thick green grass that you only found in this part of the country. Wildflowers could be found along the hills. During fall, the leaves and grass turn red, yellow, and orange, giving a beautiful view. During winter, the trees are dull in color but still a good camouflage. For the most part though this was one of my favorite places to be particularly during summertime. There was a sense of peace that I could find here.

I owned a few properties around the country, all of them tucked away from any major cities. I knew many individuals who did what I did and all of them preferred to live in big cities where they could blend in with society. I understood their way of thinking. It didn't mean I agreed with it. I never lived in a place where I was planning a job, nor did I believe blending in would keep me from being caught. If anything, it made it easier to be found and picked up on surveillance cameras, traffic cameras, or being recognized on a new report. My nearest neighbors here in Georgia were three miles away. At my other properties some were closer five miles away from my property line. It was a requirement for me to have as much distance around me as possible. On top of distance, I used a different identity with anyone who lived in the area. Locals knew I traveled and spent weeks if not months away from each property. It ensured I was protected from being turned in or anyone taking notice of me overall. I kept the houses modest in size. Mail was never sent to any of my properties and instead were sent to P.O. boxes in separate towns than where I resided. I took every precaution I could to ensure I hid in plain sight.

The other upside to picking a remote place was that the woods for me were peaceful. It was where I could think, find my peace, and just be who I truly was. I spent large chunks of my life being a number of different people. The only place I could just be me was when I was alone. My homes provided that solitude and security.

This house was a small two-bedroom house. It was no more than twelve hundred square feet with an open living room and kitchen. I had a big comfortable sofa in the living room with a television and a Blu-Ray player. I had no streaming services because they could be easily tracked. I didn't waste time having a dining room set because it was just me who lived here and I never brought anyone back to my place. The master bedroom had a large iron bed frame with a thick, soft mattress.

I had a small table to the right of the bed where I kept a book to read before I went to bed and my alarm clock. A large bathroom for one sat between the two rooms. The bathroom had a stand-alone shower and a large clawed-foot tub.

The other bedroom was turned into a workshop where I could work spells. I kept a garden on the back of my house where I grew all of my materials I needed for any spells. I spent a large amount of my time here because it was where I felt the most at home. It ensured my garden also could thrive most of the year. The front of the house had a large porch where I had a lounge chair set up with a small table to match. I loved sitting on my porch on a Sunday morning, drinking coffee and enjoying the scent of nature and quiet.

Normally, when I pulled up to my home, there was a sense of joy that filled me. Tonight, it was more of a sense of relief. I shut my car off and sighed as the events of the night replayed in my head for the tenth time. Of all the males who could have approached me, why did it have to be an art thief specialist? I didn't have long term relationships. I had flings and Jasper would have been the perfect candidate for a fling or a quick one night of fun. He was attractive, could hold a conversation, and was smart. It was all of the traits I found the most attractive.

Of course, there was the situation that another thief had been at the party tonight as well. Henry Augustus had a lot of money and a large art collection. Whoever the thief was could have wanted any of the pieces. Or at least that was what I was hoping for. If the thief stole Love and Dread, it meant I would have to watch all of the black-market sales in order to obtain it. Of course, what were the chances there were two of us in the same location hunting the same painting? How could so many things have gone wrong in one night?

I walked into my house and locked the front door behind me. I turned and leaned against the door as I tossed my heels near the sofa. I took a few deep breaths before moving away from the door. Next to go was my mask which I threw onto the sofa as I tried to let go of the night's events. The theft of the Augustus home meant I needed to move on from my plans. Whatever had happened tonight was not my problem except I couldn't let it go. I wanted the painting and whoever had assaulted the server prevented me from getting what I wanted. That irritated me.

I needed to know what had happened. I pulled my burner phone out of my purse and turned it on. I always went with pay as you go phones because they were easy to toss and get a new one if needed. I also liked them because they were harder to trace. Most companies and law enforcement agencies didn't waste their time trying. I only turned the phone on when it was necessary and as soon as I was done, I turned it off immediately.

It took the device a few seconds to boot up. I walked over and dropped myself on my sofa. I opened the search engine and began my search for any news about any assaults, current police activity, and breaking news. Nothing came up. I changed my search to police activity in Wilmington Park. Still nothing. It could have been too soon for a story to be posted but I doubted it. My guess was Jasper was keeping it out of the news. It meant it had more than likely been art the thief was after.

I changed gears and began to search for information about Jasper instead. It took me only a few minutes to find what I was looking for. There were several articles about the male retrieving artwork from several thefts across the country. All of them referred to Jasper as a human and talked about how successful he truly was as an art hunter. There was even a puff piece about the male and how he started at Icarus. I found his profile on LinkedIn even. He had worked for the insurance company for several years. He was a lead investigator. Every article referred to him as a human. The wolf was pretending to be human in order to get ahead. I wasn't mad at him for it, not in the least. It just meant that he was a little more like me than I thought. Mind you it didn't mean I could call him but it made me like him a little more. I exited my search and shut the phone down once more. I pulled his card from my purse and ran my finger along the edge as I stared at his name. He was handsome, smart, and understood art. There was something about the male that made me want to have more time with him. Jasper was pulling a beautiful con over a group of humans who protected the rich. Damn, I wish I could have just one night of conversation with him, maybe sex even but I couldn't. I lived a life that didn't allow for that. I stood up and walked into the kitchen. I looked at his business card one more time, wishing he was a different male.

"Maybe in the next life we could have our fun." I said to the universe.

I tossed the card into the trash can and headed for my bedroom. It had been a long night that ended with me missing a chance at having my painting. It was time to curl up in my bed and sleep.

Chapter Three

I slept for a while until my brain began to work through what my next move was. I rolled over seeing that it was four a.m. I cursed at the time and my brain seemed to have grown bored with sleeping. I stayed in bed, tossing and turning for a little while longer until I finally accepted, I was not going back to sleep. I climbed out of bed and headed to the kitchen. I filled the coffee maker with water and coffee grounds and hit brew. I moved to the fridge and pulled out two eggs and began to make my breakfast. I broke the yolk and added pepper and garlic to the eggs as the burner heated up. I waited for the eggs to start to fry and tossed bread into the toaster. It took about two more minutes for the eggs to finish frying. I buttered my toast and placed the egg on the plate I kept beside the stove. I set my plate to the side and grabbed a mug from the cabinet. As I went through the motions, I replayed the events from the night before. Jasper came to mind first but I pushed it away moving forward. He was not important to the story, I told my brain. I replayed everything I had witnessed trying to find clues. I should be moving forward, start searching for a new job but it was hard to walk away from a piece I wanted as badly as I did.

I added some creamer to the bottom of the mug and waited for the coffee maker to finish its job. It took a few more minutes for it to finish. I poured coffee into the mug and carried everything into the living room. I set the mug next to the sofa and began to eat. I turned on the television and hit play on the Blu-Ray player. I couldn't remember what I had left in the Blu-Ray player. It took only a few moments for the movie to start. Be Cool came on the screen about twenty minutes into the movie. I ate and watched as John Travolta began playing all sides of the situation. I sat and laughed at the movie. I had watched it more than was probably healthy but it was a movie that asked nothing from me and it allowed me to just enjoy the quietness of my life.

I finished eating and paused the movie. I took a sip of coffee before I made my way to the kitchen. I washed my dishes as my brain began to wonder again. I needed to look and see what the media was reporting. Someone had to talk to the media. There would be something in the news but it wouldn't have a lot of information.

I finished the dishes and turned off the movie. I retrieved my phone from the bedroom and headed back to the living room. I turned the phone on once more and began my search. It took only moments to find an article about the attempted robbery. I read through the short article. The story that the media had was that a man had become violent at a charity event. He had attacked a member of the waitstaff before escaping. There was a brief description of the man but nothing more.

I moved onto the next article getting the same information as the first. I headed to the next best source of information, a broker of the underworld so to say. I dialed his number from memory. It rang twice.

"Password?" A female voice spoke.

"Five-Three-Eight-One." I answered.

Each client of The Broker had a password in order to be able to speak to him. He dealt with only certain individuals and I was one of his best clients.

"Hold, please."

I sat waiting for a minute before the rough voice of the broker came on.

"Red. How are you? Have a new piece for me to auction?"

"Not exactly. I need information."

There was a pause.

"You know I don't give information for free." He reminded me.

"I'm well aware of that."

"What can you offer me?" The Broker asked.

I had a few pieces I kept on hand for moments like this.

"The Denmark Mermaid statue?" I offered.

"Bronze?"

"Yes."

"It is worth only between ten to twenty-thousand. I am not sure it is enough."

The Broker was trying to weasel more from me. The problem was I knew his game.

"As one of your top clients, I believe the statue will be enough."

"Red..."

"Do not play with me or I can always find a new broker to go through. I believe The Mediator has been looking for new clients." I threatened.

"You think you can get what I make for you or give you information the way I do?"

"I don't know but if I go to him, it means you lose the best business you have."

"I can always find another you." The Broker countered.

"No, you can find another client but not one as good as I am."

"You wouldn't go with him after all this time, would you?" The Broker questioned me.

I smiled, knowing I had him.

"I will if you continue to fuck with me. All I need to know is about the attempted theft in Savannah last night. It is your choice if you take my offer or not."

I waited for his answer.

"This is why I love you, Red. You are always a ball buster." The Broker laughed.

"Is that a yes?"

"It is. River Street Market, one p.m. Password is Six-Four-Nine-Two."

"Thank you, Broker." I said before hanging up.

It was time to enjoy my coffee and finish my movie.

Chapter Four

The hours leading up to the meet up, I spent looking for my next project. I logged onto my computer. I had a small laptop that I kept hidden in a nook in the house. I only used the computer for no more than an hour or two at the most and I ran all of my searches through a proxy or technically through several proxies to ensure I kept my searches from triggering any watch list. My internet service was provided by a local company with just the basic needs. Most days the router was off except for when I needed it.

I began to search for artwork that had been moved into private collections. It took me a matter of minutes to find what I was looking for. The thing with the wealthy and today's society is everyone loves to brag about what they have. The general public enjoys showing off how happy they were, the mess of their lives, and every little piece of themselves. The wealthy love doing the same thing but they loved flaunting their money and what it could buy them. A few keystrokes were all it took. I found one of the paintings, Grain Stacks by Monet. It was an oil painting that was created somewhere around 1890. It was of two haystacks in a field at sunrise. It wasn't an exciting painting but it was one that had a beautiful texture to it. There were a total of fifteen pieces to the set. They each hung side by side telling the story of the haystacks. The painting I was looking at resided in upstate New York as of nine months ago. It was a piece that few would care about even the insurance company, making it easy to steal and do as I wish with it.

I began to dig through more about the painting and its history. It had been on display in Europe until about a year ago. Museums in Europe are not allowed to sell pieces to private collectors but they are allowed to transfer the object to another museum. In the United

States though, museums can sell any piece of artwork they own to whoever they wish. It was typical for museums to sell art after they had displayed it for a certain period of time in order to make room for new pieces. The Haystack paintings were less beautiful and boring to most art lovers.

The painting moved from Europe to a museum here for a month. It was never put on display, instead it was placed in an auction. Selling the painting would make the museum money to be able to buy better pieces. All of the collection was transferred to a museum in New York. From there, all of the pieces were sold at auction for millions of dollars. I wanted all of the paintings but I didn't know if that was possible. All fifteen paintings were sold to different collectors. To be able to collect them all would take years. I would have to spread out each job over several years. The best I could do right now was research the painting that still resided in New York.

I switched my search to the new owner. His name was Laurence Mayweather. He was raised wealthy and had added to the family wealth by diving into real estate. He was planning an event in a month that would not just display Monet, but other art within his collection. The event was a charity event with a silent auction. Chances were good that meant artwork was going to be auctioned off. He would give three percent of the profits to charity and the rest would go to Mr. Mayweather. The event would be a perfect opportunity to retrieve the painting.

I cleared the computer's search and began to think of all my options. I shut the computer down and the router. I wanted Love and Pain more than I have ever wanted another painting but making a move on it would be dangerous. Jasper and his huntner Silas would be in the middle of their investigation into what happened last night. It would take a few days to close the case. It would be another month for any payout to Henry Augustus. By then, Henry would be ready for another party. Jasper would more than likely be in attendance. It would be easy to wait a few months and try again. I could go to upstate New York and see what I was dealing with in terms of security and if it was at all possible to get my hands on one of the paintings.

It was a good plan but one I hated. The need to have the second painting of Edvard Munch's was like an addiction for me. I had been stalking that painting for years and I finally had the opportunity to get it, only to have it slip through my grasp because of a C class thief. Walking away pissed me off, even if it was only for a few months. Anything in that time could happen to it. It could be sold, damaged, or even stolen by someone else. If the last happened, I would be angry with myself for letting it slip away.

The responsible thing would be to move forward and try again at another time. I reasoned with myself that I was going to do the right thing. I would see what the Broker contact knew from the night before and then I would pack up and head to New York.

I SHOWERED AND DRESSED a few hours later. The drive to Savannah would take longer than it did last night just because it was the middle of the day. Once I arrived, I would have to find parking close enough to walk to and far enough away that most wouldn't take notice of the vehicle I was driving. The River Market is busy and can be crowded in the afternoon. It made it easier to blend in but it also made it more difficult for parking and traveling through.

I arrived and parked a block away from the market. Humans and hellborns were out, enjoying life with the sun shining bright. The humidity was high once more as I climbed from my car. Today, I had my hair pulled back in a ponytail. I was in a black tank top, jeans, and a Braves baseball cap. My black sunglasses completed my look. I had the statue in a brown bag with handles that looked to have come from any of the stores or vendors in the area. I kept my head low as I moved down the street, scanning the area. It took a few minutes for me to reach the bench in the front of the market. There was no one there yet which meant I could wander through the market before I met the contact.

The River Street Market ran along the Seneca and Tugaloo River. There were several other businesses in the area. There were shops and restaurants with outdoor seating. An old-fashioned ice cream shop sat just down the road. The biggest attraction was the actual market building. It was an open-air building with no doors or true windows. There were multiple vendors set up in small spaces. Vendors selling jewelry, clothing, and snacks. I walked through, watching as people shopped and bargained with vendors. I stopped and admired a few jewelry stands, never staying at one booth longer than necessary. I weaved through the rows of vendors, exiting from the other side.

I still had time to kill so I headed to the ice cream shop. I ordered a scoop of chocolate ice cream with no toppings. I paid in cash and headed back down the street. I scanned the area as I moved. I had asked for the meeting but it didn't mean that The Broker wouldn't set me up if he got into a tight spot. Most law enforcement suck at blending into the crowd. The higher the cop goes in terms of rank the worse they are at blending in.

Once I was confident that there were no cops in the area, I headed to the meeting. There were two benches sitting outside the market. I picked the one on the right and sat down. I angled myself so I could rest my right elbow on the back of the bench. I sat the paper bag down next to me and waited. I ate my ice cream as I scanned the area. Two minutes passed when an older woman in a yellow summer dress and a big cream-colored hat sat down next to me.

"Hello Dear." She greeted me.

I gave her a nod of my head.

"Hello." I said evenly.

"Such a beautiful day isn't it." The woman turned to face me. She leaned forward and whispered "Password?"

This was the Broker's informant.

"Six-Four-Nine-Two." I spoke quietly as I finished my ice cream. I sat the cup down on the bench next to me.

"You may call me Granny." The woman said under her breath.

I smiled.

"How are you doing today, Granny?" I asked.

"It is a little warmer today than I thought it would be but not as hot as it could be."

She was talking in code. Weather referred to law enforcement and investigators.

"At least it isn't raining, yet."

"It's interesting you say that. I have a friend named Gunner who loves the rain but is never prepared for it. He believes he's a lot smarter than he truly is."

This was what I was looking for. Gunner was the name of a thief who wasn't nearly as good as I was nor was he as smart as he thought he was. He believed he was the best, which made him arrogant and foolish in his decision making. Gunner took risks most successful thieves wouldn't bother with. I had few dealings with the thief and I never bought any of his art pieces because I didn't trust him.

"It can be hard getting caught in the rain if it's coming down hard enough."

"Yes, it can be. From what I hear, he was caught in a bit of a storm the other night and now he is paying the price for being underprepared."

"Was he injured?" I asked.

"Minor injuries. His friend came out with no injuries and clear of any bad weather."

Gunner had a partner. That was out of character for the thief.

"Is he in the hospital?" I questioned.

"Yes, but not for long. He should be released this afternoon."

"And the friend?"

"Nowhere to be seen." Granny answered. His partner abandoned him. "Is that for me?"

"Possibly." I smiled and waited. I needed to know what he stole.

Granny smiled at me. She leaned forward and hugged me.

"Portrait of a Young Man and he failed to retrieve it." Granny whispered.

She released me and grabbed the bag. She looked inside it.

"It is beautiful. Thank you so much for the gift." She tucked the bag under her arm and stood up. "It was wonderful to see you. Remember, I'm just a call away if you need anything."

I gave her a nod. She turned around and headed down the street. I sat on the bench a little longer. The painting Portrait of a Young Man was a painting believed to have been destroyed during World War II. How could Henry Augustus own a lost painting? It made me curious about who Augustus was. I had done a deep dive into every piece he owned. There was no record of him owning that painting. If it was known by Icarus, he would have been required to take more precautions with his collection. There would also be museums wanting to get their hands on it. It would be big news in the art world.

It led me to start asking myself what connections did he have that no one knew about? A lost painting the Nazis had stolen turning up meant it had been passed through people connected to the Nazi party. Everything I had learned about Augustus didn't tie him to any hate groups or anyone who would be tied to someone in question about their family. To get his hands on that painting told me he had connections to illegal activity.

My thoughts moved to Jasper. Did Icarus know he had a stolen painting dating back to World War II? What did Gunner tell law enforcement he was after? Who was he working with? Or was it that Gunner was working for someone. Granny had said he had a partner but was it a job he was hired for?

I stood up and began to move down the street toward my car. I found a nearby trash can and tossed my ice cream cup into the trash can. I wasn't paying as close of attention as I should have been when I bumped into a male.

"I'm so sorry." The male began to say until he looked at who he was talking to. "Kathrine?"

Shit! It was Jasper. There were over one hundred thousand people in Savannah and that didn't include tourists and of all the hellborns to run into in the middle of Savannah I found Jasper. I smiled softly as I looked at the male. He was just as attractive as he had been the night before. Today, he was in a black t-shirt that hugged his arms. I could see how defined they were. His arms were chiseled with a large tattoo poking out on his left arm from under his sleeve. There was no way he didn't work out with the size that he was. His dark blue jeans fit nicely around his hips. I took notice of his flat stomach. A pair of black sneakers and a paperboy hat completed his look today. Not everyone could pull off the paperboy hat but Jasper could. It gave him a bad boy look.

"Jasper." I had no idea how I was going to get out of this.

"How are you?"

Jasper smiled at me as his eyes moved slowly down my body.

"I'm good."

"I wish we could have spent more time talking last night. In fact, I tried to find you once everything calmed down."

My brain worked quickly.

"I wanted to as well but I had an early morning." I answered.

There was a moment that passed between us, one that said he was just as interested in me as I was in him.

"I thought you were heading out today?"

"I was supposed to first thing this morning but my flight got canceled." I lied.

Jasper smiled at me.

"That sucks for your plans but it means I can ask you to lunch now."

"What?" I asked confused.

"My client has agreed to have no more events for the next few months which means my role here is done for now. You are here because your flight was canceled so why don't we take this opportunity to get some lunch before we both head our separate ways."

I wanted to say no because of the risk this male posed to my life but I also wanted to spend time with him. Jasper and I had spent only ten minutes at the most talking but there was something about him that I liked. I wanted to get to know him. I knew how stupid that sounded. It could only end with me running from him and yet I found myself truly wanting more time with him.

"Okay."

Jasper's smile grew wider.

"Where would you like to go?" Jasper asked me.

"I'm picking?"

"Do you not live here? You should know where there is a good place to go around here."

"I visit here more than live but lucky for you I know where we can go." I said.

I forced Jasper to turn around and headed down the street. He walked beside me, glancing at me as we walked.

"So where do you live?"

"I don't have what most would consider a home. I am always on the move which means I am only in one location for no more than a couple of weeks before I head to the next place."

"Is the wine business that good?" Jasper asked.

"Yes and no. If I want to build my business to its fullest extent, I have to work all the time," I answered.

I didn't deal in wine as he believed but I did have a thriving business technically. I worked all the time to make sure I had what I needed and to ensure I was successful. Traveling was part of that.

"Seems lonely. What about your family?"

"It's just me so it makes it easy to keep moving." I answered honestly. I pointed to the restaurant two doors down from where we were. "Belford's is the best or they are in my opinion."

We walked down to the restaurant. He opened the door for me. I stepped inside, feeling the air conditioning hit me. He followed me inside.

"Welcome to Belford. How many are in your party?"

"Two, please." I spoke to the hostess.

The woman looked down the list of tables that were available.

"Would you prefer inside or on the patio?"

I looked at Jasper who was scanning the restaurant the same way I did. Inside meant less people would see us but limited a quick exit. Outside gave me more options and I could watch the people of the city.

"Patio." I answered.

"Right this way." The hostess led us through the restaurant and onto the patio. The table was small and sat against the railing, giving us a view of the water and the street. I sat on one side of the table where I could see the restaurant while Jasper took the other. The hostess handed us the menus. "Your waiter will be with you shortly."

She left us as we began to look over the menu.

"What do you recommend?" Jasper asked me.

"Personally, I like the shrimp po'boy."

Jasper looked at me and smiled.

"I did not expect that response."

"Why, because of where we met?"

"Yes."

"Just because I was at an expensive party doesn't mean that I can't enjoy simpler things, nor does it mean I only like expensive or lavish things."

Jasper stared at me for a moment.

"You are an interesting female." Jasper looked at me.

"How are we today?" Our waiter placed two water glasses down on the table. He pulled a tablet out from under his arm. "Do we still need a few minutes to decide what we are having?"

"Yes, we do." Jasper answered.

"I'll be back in a moment."

The waiter walked away. I looked back at the menu.

"How do you feel about ordering a couple of appetizers?" I asked.

"You want just an appetizer?" Jasper almost seemed confused by my suggestion.

"I am not that hungry and I do have to get ready to head out to my next destination. I prefer to eat lighter before I travel."

"Okay. What were you thinking?"

"Fried Green Tomatoes and Calamari."

"I agree with the calamari but not the tomatoes." Jasper cringed at the word.

"Not a fan of tomatoes?" I asked.

"Not in the least. How about we do the crab cakes?"

I chuckled.

"I wouldn't say that is exactly a light meal."

"Crab is light." Jasper retorted.

"Not when it's fried."

"You were willing to do the fried tomatoes," Jasper challenged me.

I smirked at him.

"Fine. Let's do it but I'm ordering biscuits."

A few minutes later the waiter returned so we could order. Jasper and I sat and talked; our conversation flowed easily. It felt like we had known each other for years instead of for a day. We talked about everything from sports, to places we both had traveled. It turned out Jasper worked as much as I did. He had no family or pack, which was unlike most wolves. Most couldn't thrive on their own. I was guessing it made it easier for him to hide what he truly was. Jasper tried to ensure he made time to see whatever city he was visiting, making his job more enjoyable. I did the same thing, mind you mine was more to ensure that I knew all of the weak points of the city. It didn't mean I didn't find hidden treasures in each city I visited.

Jasper was as smart as I believed he was. He had started at the bottom of the company, answering the phones, making coffee, and taking orders from executives. Jasper worked his way through the company, making a name for himself for the past eight years. Once he became an investigator, climbing the corporate ladder was easy. He learned from every investigator how to be the best until he reached the top.

For the most part, he worked solo up until a year ago. Silas had been an investigator for the past four years never making big strides as Jasper had done. The bosses wanted Silas to learn from Jasper and had paired them up. He didn't say it but I could tell he was not impressed with the human.

As guarded as I was about my life, I found myself opening up to Jasper. I never let him know about being a thief but other parts of my life I freely shared.

"What's the best place you have ever traveled to?" Jasper asked me.

I paused as I thought about his question.

"New Orleans." I answered.

"New Orleans?"

"Yes, New Orleans."

"You do realize that most would not pick New Orleans. Between the hurricanes and the crime rates most would pick a place like Paris."

"I know, but I love the feel of the city. There is so much history, music, and art that you can see only in New Orleans. There is nothing like it. I'm not into the nightlife but the daytime is just full of energy." He smiled at me. "What about you?"

"Rome in the summertime. For the exact same reasons as why you love New Orleans."

Rome was a city I had always wanted to travel to but didn't because it required a plane ticket. I tried to ensure that there were few things that could be traced to me. I didn't want an electronic footpath if I could avoid it. Flights were one of those things that created a problem for me. Flying internationally meant I needed a passport which allowed the government to research my background. Going to an airport meant I would have to deal with facial recognition software taking images of me, being able to scan me and search my luggage. I wanted none of that in my life.

"I've not been to Rome. Tell me about it."

"The city is hot in the middle of the day but the things you can see there are amazing. The buildings that have been standing for centuries are constructed with a perfection that we do not have today. Going to the Vatican was breathtaking. I have spent my entire career dealing with art and that place is like one big piece of art." Jasper described his experience. "If you get tired of the city, not far from Rome is a cliff city that has crystal clear water and is peaceful. If that isn't enough you can catch a train to another city that is just as beautiful."

"How many times have you been to Rome?"

"Twice."

I wasn't going to lie, I was a little jealous of him at that moment. Being a thief was who I was. It allowed me to see the United States. I was able to touch paintings no one else would get to. On the other side of that, I couldn't hop a plane to anywhere I wanted to. I didn't get to meet and spend time with someone like Jasper. I was alone. Most days, I didn't mind it but moments like this I did.

By the time we finished eating it was late afternoon. Jasper paid the bill and we left together.

"Thank you for having lunch with me." Jasper said as we stood on the street.

"I had fun, Jasper."

He leaned forward, dropping his head slightly. He smelled like fresh trees and wild

flowers, a scent I knew well. It was the scent of my home here in Georgia. I couldn't resist myself. I kissed Jasper and wrapped my arms around his neck. He wrapped his arms around my waist and kissed me back. I loved the feeling of being pressed against his body which made the kiss even better.

Jasper ended our kiss and looked at me.

"Would it be too forward to ask you who's place we could go to?" Jasper asked me.

The smart play would be to say neither but that kiss had been unlike anything I had ever experienced. I wanted him, which made me stupid.

"Not in the least. Where are you staying?"

"The Hyatt." Jasper answered me before he kissed me again. This time only giving me his lips. My need for him grew. I wanted to see him naked. I wanted his lips on my body.

"My car's down the street." I replied.

"Let's go."

I slid my hand into his and led him to my car.

Chapter Five

It took us ten minutes to get to the hotel. I parked my car in the hotel parking garage. Jasper held out his hand as I came around the vehicle. I was trying to avoid the feeling of belonging to him. His large hand and my small one felt like we were made for one another. It was a feeling I had never had before. I tried to ignore the feeling.

We walked through the lobby. The space had grey walls with white, grey and black fake marble floors. Bright lights hung above us, lighting every inch of the space. Soft off-white chairs were set up in pairs throughout the wide lobby. I could see a bar at the opposite end. There were a few people sitting in the lobby talking softly. Jasper didn't pause as he led me past the front desk and to the elevator. As we approached the elevator, the door opened as if they were waiting for us. There were several individuals who stepped off the elevator one at a time. Conversation began as they headed for the doors. Jasper guided us onto the elevator and hit the button for the twelfth floor. He waited for the door to close before he turned to face me. He pulled me against him, kissing me. Jasper slipped his tongue into my mouth without any hesitation. I kissed him back, our tongues moving with one another. I couldn't resist him. Jasper pushed me against the wall of the elevator. I felt his hard cock through his jeans as he kissed me. He released my mouth, moving to my neck. My body tightened with excitement. Before I could respond with more than a moan. The elevator slowed. There was a soft noise. We looked at the digital counter, we were only on the sixth floor. Jasper placed me in front of him as humans and hellborns stepped onto the elevator. He held me against him, his erection pressed up against me. We waited as the elevator moved slowly through the floors stopping at two separate floors. The elevator ride gave me the time to rethink my decision of what I was doing. I liked Jasper more than I should have. Our lunch date had been fun as we joked and got to know one another but he was a threat to my lifestyle. What was I thinking? He was a male who hunted individuals like me. I glanced at Jasper who looked at me with hungry eyes. The look in those eyes and the feel of his cock pressed against me, aching to be inside of me pushed all my reasons away.

The elevator slowed once more announcing our arrival at our floor. He took my hand in his and turned to the left. We walked quickly down the hall. We reached the end of the hall and turned again. Jasper stopped at the last door that was placed near the stairwell and pulled out a key card. He pushed the door open and allowed me to walk in first.

As soon as we were inside, Jasper shut and locked the door. I pulled my hat off and tossed it on the side table with my sunglasses. We stared at each other for only a moment before he moved towards me. Jasper grabbed a hold of my waist and pulled me to him. Our lips met and that was it. Our desire for one another took hold. We were both lost to it. I broke our kiss as I pulled his shirt over his head, tossing it to the side. I looked at his bare chest seeing just how built he was. His shoulders were wide with perfectly sculpted muscles. His wide chest had hair that covered his pecs and traveled down into a thin line of hair over his abs. I was not a female who normally enjoyed a man with hair on his chest but with Jasper, it didn't seem to matter. It was my turn to pull him to me and kiss him. It was all Jasper needed. He kissed me deeply as our tongues met. Jasper's arms wrapped around my body as we kissed. The feel of my body pressed against his felt like I belonged there just as it had felt with my hand in his. We moved closer to the bed as one, his hand moved under my shirt pulling it off of me. Our movement with one another wasn't awkward or clumsy. It was as if we knew how the other was going to move. I had been with other males for nothing more than a one-night stand. They were a good time but it was always off, never more than that. Jasper was different.

I felt as he tried to heel toe his sneakers off. He was struggling which forced him to stop kissing me. I stepped back away from him and took my shoes off. Jasper did the same as soon as they were off Jasper grabbed ahold of the back of my neck and pulled me to him once more. He kissed me harshly as he angled us towards the bed. One minute we were standing, the next we were on the bed. I felt as Jasper's ground his pelvis against mine. I moaned into his mouth wanting nothing to be between us.

I pushed Jasper over to the left; he gave me what I wanted as he rolled onto his back holding me to him. I kissed him for another moment before I undid my bra. I stood up and stripped out of my shorts. Jasper watched me as I undressed. His eyes trailed down my body. His green eyes were brighter than normal. I leaned down and undid the button on his jeans. He pulled his jeans off with his boxers. I stood and took in every inch of his body. He was the most beautiful piece of art I had ever seen. Jasper's body was well sculpted with beautiful lines of muscles along every inch of his body. His cock was long and thick and curved up towards his belly. I wanted to know what it felt like to take him in my mouth before I rode him. I wanted his mouth on every inch of my body. I wanted to feel him come deep inside of me as I orgasmed with him.

Jasper sat up and took my hand pulling me onto the bed. I sat next to him as I ran my hand down the center of his body. My nails brush across his skin softly. Goose bumps spread along his flesh. I found the tip of his cock. I gripped him firmly and began to stroke him slowly. I watched Jasper's face as he moaned softly. His eyes closed as I played with him. I moved down the bed and climbed over his legs. My movement made him open his eyes. I looked at Jasper as I bent down and took him in my mouth. He moaned louder as I sucked on him.

"Yes, god yes!" Jasper's words made me want to come.

I didn't stop as I took all of his cock in my mouth. His hand grabbed my head as his pelvis began to move. I felt as he touched the back of my throat. I let my eyes roll up, finding Jasper was watching me. I sucked on him harder as I moved up and down him. His eyes never leaving my face. I felt as he came. I slid down his cock one final time allowing his seed to spill down my throat. I pulled him from my mouth and looked up at Jasper. He was panting. I smiled loving the taste of him and the pleasure I was able to give him. I began to stroke his cock. I wanted to feel every inch of his inside of me.

I stroked him only for a few minutes before I moved back up towards him. I swung my leg over his body. I arched my back as I placed my hands on either side of his head and leaned up. I angled my lower body, so his cock was pressed just outside of my opening. I slid just the tip of him inside of me, moving slowly down his shaft. The feeling of him inside of me caused me to gasp. He was at the end of me and yet I could feel as his cock pushed farther into me. Jasper looked up at me as I moved my hips back and forth. It didn't take long for me to come. Every stroke hit that spot deep inside of me. I moaned as I continued to sway my hips stroking his cock with my core. Jasper wrapped his arms around me and tilted his head up. He captured my nipple in his mouth as I rode his body. He sucked slowly at first but I felt his desire to do so much more. He sucked harder as I began to come once more. Jasper released my nipple and looked up at me. I watched him as he stuck his tongue out and licked my other nipple before he pulled it into his mouth. I called his name as I held his head to my body. I moved faster, coming quicker and harder than before. Jasper released my breath and stared up at me.

"I guess that makes you mine now." Jasper whispered.

His words made me fuck him harder. I slammed my body down on his repeatedly, feeling every inch of him over and over again. It wasn't enough. I needed him deeper inside of me. I rolled my hips faster as I had my way with him. I moaned louder with each orgasm. I looked down at him and saw Jasper had placed his arms under his head as he watched me come. I could see the enjoyment on his face as he watched me.

"You are so beautiful." Jasper's voice was rough as he spoke.

I was stunned at his words. No one had ever spoken to me like that, especially during sex.

"I need you deep inside of me," I panted.

I moved faster and harder. I felt as my body was on the verge of another release. Jasper moved his hips under me more aggressively causing me to bounce on top of him. He reached up and pulled me down against his body as he took control. He held me against him as he slammed into me. I began to yell his name as I came hard around him. Jasper growled low in my ear which drove me farther over the edge. It only took a second later for Jasper to come with me. He kept his arms around me as we both tried to learn how to breathe normally.

"That was…" I panted.

"Better than anything you've ever had?"

"Yeah."

I looked at him with a smile.

"Me too."

I kissed him knowing this was different and had no idea how I was going to walk away from this male. I pushed the thought away as if it wasn't the reality of the situation.

Chapter Six

Jasper and I lay in bed with one another. His arm rested under my shoulders, holding me close to him. There was a feeling of peace that I had never felt before. I didn't cuddle or stay longer than it took to get dressed after sex. The fact I was in his arms, pressed against his chest said how I felt for this male.

"I wish we had more time together." Jasper said, breaking the silence.

"I do too."

There was a sadness in my voice that I didn't expect to hear.

"We could meet somewhere. We both travel. Maybe there is somewhere we could meet that is a middle ground for both of us."

There was a hint of hopefulness in his voice. I wanted to say yes. I wanted more conversation, more time with him, more of this. But it wasn't possible.

"Jasper, do you truly believe we can be more than this?" I moved slightly so I could look at him.

"Why couldn't it be more?"

I lifted my head off of his arm and rolled onto my stomach.

"You and I both live a nomadic life, Jasper."

"And?" Jasper questioned me.

"We have created lives that do not allow for long lasting connections. How could we make this work?"

Jasper placed his hand on the side of my face.

"You and I are different from most hellborns. Why not try and see where this goes? I'm not asking for you to marry me just to see if we can make this work," Jasper suggested. The reason was simple but not one I could say out loud. I was the individual he hunted for a living and he was the one I hid from. And yet here I was with no desire to walk away from him. "There is no reason for us to not try."

There was something in the look he was giving me, I couldn't resist. "Okay."

Jasper leaned up and kissed me with his hand on the side of my neck. The kiss was all it took for my body to respond. I rolled over as Jasper rolled over on his side. His hand slid down my neck, along my body. My body responded as I arched up wanting more of his touch. His fingertips brushed my hips and moved down to the center of my thighs. I spread my legs for him. Jasper brushed my clit making me end our kiss with a gasp. He moved his finger slowly, teasing my clit. I looked up at Jasper seeing he was watching me intently. His fingers moved lower, finding my slit. His fingers into me slowly. I moaned as Jasper began to play with me. He watched my face as my body began to respond to his touch. My hips moved with the motion of his hand. It didn't take long for him to get me to come.

"I want to taste you." Jasper growled.

"Yes." I panted. "Please, Jasper."

He pulled his fingers from me. I watched him suck my juices from his fingers. Jasper's eyes were heavy with need. The sight of him sucking the taste of me from his fingers was a whole new level of yes please. My body tightened as my desire rose to a peak that I had never felt before. Jasper sat up and moved between my legs. He grabbed a hold of my hips and lifted me up to his face as he leaned forward. He began to lick and suck my pussy not even pausing to take it slow. The wolf knew what he was doing as he ate me out. I held onto the edge of the bed as his tongue entered me aggressively. His tongue was even better than his fingers were. The orgasms came in wave after wave making me beg for more from him. He didn't stop, instead he used his fingers to tease my clit as he used his tongue to fuck me. I wanted to watch him but couldn't do it. My orgasms were so intense I thought I was going to come apart at the seams.

Jasper looked up at me as he wiped his face. He lowered my body and entered my body with his cock. This was not just sex or fucking this was a claiming of sorts and I didn't care. I wanted him, all of him. Everything else be damned. Jasper slammed his cock into me over and over again as I yelled his name. His eyes went from watching my face as I came to watching as his dick entered me and my pussy came around him. I became lost in every feeling of the two of us together as our bodies and souls seem to meld into one.

Chapter Seven

Jasper and I had sex for another two hours. By the time we finished we were exhausted. I fell asleep in his arms taking in the scent of me on his body. There was peace in knowing I had found a male who wanted me and only me. Unfortunately for me, it couldn't last. I awoke around three a.m. feeling sore in all the right ways. I rolled over looking at the wolf wanting him more than I had ever wanted any piece of art. He was beautiful and the thought of leaving him hurt my soul but I had a decision to make. If I stayed and waited for him to wake up, I wouldn't have the strength to walk away. I gave him one more look and climbed out of the bed. I turned on the bathroom light and began to search for my clothes and shoes. I could feel the ache in my body but it was one I enjoyed. One I had never felt before. I collected all of my clothes and dressed in the bathroom. I looked at myself in the mirror knowing this was crazy. I had lost my mind to even want to be with this male. I was made for the life I had built. I wasn't designed to be with anyone. And yet, I stared at myself in the mirror wanting to cry because I could not see him ever again. I tried to ignore the feeling of sorrow as I ran my fingers through my hair quickly before I crept out of the bathroom. I found paper and a pen in the small desk in the corner of the room. I apologized for leaving. I tried to put the pen down and walk out of the room but felt the pull of not wanting to say goodbye. My heart seemed to take over as my hand scribbled down my number at the bottom of the note. I placed it on my pillow and kissed him on the cheek. He stirred slightly, turning his head to face me so he could kiss me still asleep. I gave him a quick kiss and he drifted back off to sleep. I moved quietly through the hotel room and headed to the elevator.

My head and heart were in a battle with one another. My head was saying I was a fool to have agreed to see him and an even bigger fool for leaving my number. My heart, on the other hand, was jumping for joy. If you had asked me a month ago about my life I would have said being alone was a perfect life. I had no one that could cross me or screw me out of what I truly loved. Now I wasn't so sure that was true. Jasper Wolf was different. He was living a lie just as I did everyday. He pretended to be human in order to get ahead. He had no one and counted on no one. He was a male version of me which made him the perfect male.

I now needed to decide what was my next move. Did I continue to steal and spend the time getting to know Jasper? I could meet him in another city and have nights like these before I moved on to another place, another painting, or sculpture while he caught thieves like me. Eventually Jasper would be hunting me. What did I do then?

I could walk away from what I did and start living on the straight and narrow? What did that even look like? Me being his mate having a home with him. I wasn't sure I could do that? I wasn't someone who wanted the house and family type of female.

The third option was to walk away from Jasper? I could walk away from him and continue to live the life I have always loved. Was he worth throwing everything away for? What if it all came crashing down? He didn't even know my real name. How could he want to be with someone like me?

As I thought through each of my options, I stopped paying less attention to my surroundings. I was almost to my car when I heard a voice behind me.

"Hello Red." a voice spoke from behind me.

I turned to see Silas standing behind me. His hands in his pockets as he moved slowly between the cars. My heart stopped as he said my thief name.

"How did..."

He smiled slowly as he walked towards me.

"Oh, I know you well, Red. I have studied your work for a long time. Your flawless entry techniques, your ability to blend into any crowd. You could say I admire your skills and all you have taken. Mind you, your ability to get to pieces before me has become an irritation in my life but we all have our flaws. Don't you agree?"

I didn't understand what he was saying. I cocked my head to the side.

"What do you mean?"

"I mean you have stolen a few of the pieces that I wanted. Most have never been seen again once you had them."

"You're a thief!" I began to understand what was happening.

He laughed at me.

"The look on your face is spectacular." I could see the enjoyment he was feeling. "Yes, I am. I bet you're wondering how that is possible. Let me explain. My position allows me exclusive access to all the best paintings and to remove my competition."

If I disliked Silas before, I really couldn't stand him now. I began to take in his appearance. He was in black jeans and a dark colored T-shirt. His black boots were dull in color but I was guessing they were his favorite. He had a large buck knife on his hip. Silas moved slowly towards me.

"What's your name?" I asked.

"Jager." He smiled at his own name.

I closed my eyes at the name. It was Huntsman in german. It was a name I knew but hadn't heard in about a year. The Huntsman had a reputation for doing jobs dirty. He didn't care about using violence to get what he wanted or using people to get to specific pieces. I had heard rumors of The Huntsman crossing other thieves but nothing I could confirm. An ugly thought formed in my head.

"Does Jasper know? Is he part of this?" I narrowed my eyes.

"Mr. Rockstar himself? No, he has no idea who I am or you. Mind you, he has been the problem in all my plans for the last year. It's why I haven't been able to do any jobs. You see, I had the perfect set up. Every little bit of knowledge on every piece of art from private collections to pieces in museums. If I wanted something, I could get all the information I need, boost the piece, and move on. For a while, it worked well until one of the directors within Icarus became suspicious of my extracurricular activities so they assigned him to be my partner. It forced me to stop stealing. As you know, giving up thievery is not easy. It forced me to get creative. That is where you come in Red." The Huntsman body was almost touching mine.

I did not like the sound of that.

"What do you mean where I come in?"

"Well you see, Augustus has a painting..."

The dots began to connect in my brain.

"Portrait of a Young Boy?" I asked.

The Huntsman smiled at me.

"I should have known you would know about it." The Huntsman taunted.

"You tried to get Gunner to steal it."

"I did get Gunner to steal it or to try to. As you already know, he failed. You are now going to steal it for me. I'll tell you where it is hiding it and everything you need to know about the security. You will acquire it for me, no questions asked.."

I took a step away from him.

"Why would I do that?"

"Because if you don't, I will ruin you and the male you just spent your afternoon fucking." My heart stopped at his words. "Yes, I have been watching you all day. From what I could see, you and Jasper really do have chemistry. Was he as good as you made it sound or was it an act?"

"You want the painting fine, I'll get it for you, but Jasper has nothing to do with this..."

"Oh, but he does. If I'm right about you and your wolf which, by the look on your face, tells me I am, you will want to save him. No one at Icarus knows what Jasper is and if they find out, he will lose everything. If you decide to double cross me or to not help me that information will be released to all of Icarus. I will also ensure he knows exactly who you are as I drag you off to jail. While you sit behind bars, I will spend my days hunting your private collection and taking it all. I will then sell them off to whichever collector wants them for the highest price. "

You could see the excitement in his face as he informed me.

"And how do I know you won't do that after I finish the job?"

The Huntsman raised his hand as if he was giving me an oath.

"I swear, Red, that I will leave you with your wolf as long as you get me my painting." The Huntsman placed his hand over his heart as he spoke. He couldn't help but laugh at the end.

"No. I need some sort of reassurance that you will hold your end up."

"You will just have to trust me, Red." The Huntsman brushed a hand down my arm.

I gave him a look of hatred. I either helped this piece of shit steal a painting that was probably worth millions of dollars or he would ruin everything I had built and Jasper. If it had been just me I would have contemplated walking any and telling him to fuck off but Jasper didn't deserve to have his life ruined. I couldn't do that as long as he was planning on hurting Jasper. I didn't have a choice.

"Fine."

"Good." He reached into the front pocket of his jeans and pulled out a thumb drive. "Here is everything you need. I expect you to have the painting by the end of the week. You know, I do find it entertaining that you and the wolf have become a thing. Red and Wolf being fuck buddies."

I ignored his comment about Jasper and I.

"How do I reach you once I have the painting?" I asked.

"There is a number attached to the first document on the drive. As soon as you have it, call me and I will meet you."

"Anything else?"

"Not yet. See around Red."

The Huntsman turned and walked away as he laughed at the irony of it all.

Chapter Eight

The start of my drive was filled with anger at a level I had never felt before. The Huntsman was a thief that had no moral code, no love for the art of thieving, or for what he stole. He stole to say that he could do it and to make money. It is probably why it was so easy for him to harm others. Gunner was in jail because of The Huntsman. Now, I was in The Huntman's grasp and had no way out.

As I drove, a thought crossed my mind: how was he finding out thieves' identities? Did he find their hideouts? Did he pay off collectors within our world to learn who we were? The Broker had a large business that was supposed to ensure the safety of his clients. Turning names over to The Huntsman would destroy his business. Other collectors didn't run as clean of a business. Of course, there was a chance he was blackmailing one.

The Huntsman working for Icarus meant he had access to a database of names and images of thieves. It would provide him with several individuals but not as many as it seemed he had. How was he finding us? How did he find me? Another thought crossed my mind.

I pulled my car over and reached across to the glovebox. I found my flashlight, hopped out of the car, and began to move around the vehicle. I checked the wheel wells getting on my knees. I checked the bumpers, running my hands on the underside and back of the bumper. I moved to the passenger side of my car and lay on the ground. I shined my flashlight at the chassis of the car, checking every inch of the undercarriage I could see. There was nothing that seemed out of the ordinary. I stood up and thought about where else you could place a tracker easily on a car. Under the hood would be too hot, causing the tracker to burn and die quickly. Inside the car was my next best choice.

I climbed into the backseat of the car and searched under the backseats and the floor mats. I moved to the seats and ran my hand over the lining. I checked the back pockets of the front seats. Nothing was there. I moved to the front seat and searched the center console, the glovebox, and any other area I could think of. I found nothing. I didn't like the idea of driving my car back to my home. What if there was a tracker on my car? The only way to ensure I wasn't being tracked was to dump the car. The question became how would I get home?

I started the car and headed in a different direction from my home. I turned left at the next turn, I made another left and kept driving until I made it to the train station. I parked the car at the back of the lot where the camera would not be able to get a clear picture of me. I pocketed my keys, pulled all of the documents from the glove box, and walked away. The car was registered under one of my aliases, which I hadn't used in five years. It would be towed and within thirty days sold in an auction shortly after that. It also meant that identity was burned. I would never be able to use it again.

I began to walk through the city and to work through what I was going to do next. I needed a car, I needed to see what he had on the drive, and how I could save my ass from this fucking mess. I didn't trust The Huntsman in the least. Getting the painting was the easy part. It was what happened after. I was confident as soon as I had what he wanted, he was going to take me down and burn Jasper along the way. This was one of those moments when I wished I had a partner. I knew thieves that worked with the same partner for every job or they had a spouse who knew who they were. They shared a life with them. I always believed they were foolish because it allowed someone to have a figurative knife to your throat all the time. The part I never saw was that having a partner made it easier to ensure this didn't happen to you. Having a partner means you could double cross the person who is trying to hurt you. I didn't have that. It was why he picked me.

That thought led me to a new thought. What if I had a partner? What if I brought someone in on this. Gunner would be the best option but he was sitting in jail his entire life on the line. I ran through the list of thieves I knew. None of them I could truly trust just because I didn't know who The Huntsman had in his pocket or who else he knew. I needed someone who could not only help me steal the painting but also take out The Huntsman. There was only one I could think of and he was the one who didn't even know he was in danger, Jasper.

I turned down a side street and walked to a park. I found a bench and truly thought through the idea. Jasper knew how we thought because he hunted us and what we stole. He knew the Augustus house and the security system and any loopholes within it. He also knew The Huntsman and how he worked. He would be able to predict what The Huntsman would do next better than I could. Chances were good The Huntsman was in Icarus' system which would give us inside information.

I knew Jasper would hate the idea and possibly me if I brought him in. He would want nothing to do with my plan or what I was going to have to do but Jasper was involved whether he knew it or not. I needed someone who could help me and have the motivation to do so. The thought of telling Jasper the truth was terrifying. I liked Jasper, I could even love him. If I told him who I was, what would he do? He could have me arrested. He could try to figure out every job I had ever done to retrieve my pieces. He could just turn his back on me and walk away. Or, he could help me take The Huntsman down and walk away from me. It felt like a risk to bring Jasper in that could lead to my ending. Did I have a choice?

I kept running through every scenario. All of it ended in heartache for me but at least one could save Jasper. I took a deep breath and dialed the hotel. I went through all the prompts to get to the front desk.

"Hyatt Hotel, how may I be of assistance?" A pleasant voice asked.

"Room 1232." I asked.

"Please hold."

It took a second for the phone to ring. It rang several times until he finally answered.

"Hello?" Jasper answered, his voice was gravelly.

"Jasper."

"Katherine." There was a pause. "Where are you?"

"I need your help."

"Okay. That still doesn't answer my question."

I took a deep breath.

"I'm at a park and I need you to come get me."

"Okay, where are you?"

"Dixon Park."

"I'm on my way."

I hung up and sat there feeling defeated. My heart ached for what I was about to do. There was no way he would stay once he knew the truth.

Chapter Nine

Jasper arrived twenty minutes later. I could see the concern on his face as I climbed in the car.

"What happened?" Jasper turned in the driver's seat and brushed his hand on my cheek.

"Has Silas had access to this vehicle?" I asked.

"Katherine, what…"

"Jasper, answer the question first!"

"Yes."

"Shit!" I cursed. "It's a rental, correct?"

"Yeah." I could see the confusion on his face.

"Did you purchase the insurance policy?"

"I always do."

"Pop the hood."

I was being paranoid and I knew it. The problem was The Huntsman would have to consider that I would take this route. I would not take any chances with him. I climbed out of the car as he popped the hood. I found the fuse box and what I was looking for. I pulled the ECU fuse and damaged it. I set the fuse back in the box but didn't push it all the way in.

"What are you doing?"

I turned to Jasper and placed my hands on his chest.

"I need you to call the car rental company and tell them the car will not start. They will come get the car and give you a new one. As soon as you have a new car we can talk."

Jasper looked at me but he did what I asked. He called the rental car agency and spoke to the operator. It took ten minutes to make the arrangements for them to pick up the car. I watched as he handled everything.

"You ready to tell me what the fuck is going on?"

I MADE JASPER WAIT until the rental car company arrived and towed the other car. Jasper concocted a story about taking a run through the park. It drove fine to the location but after his run the car wouldn't start. They hooked up the car to the truck and drove us to the nearest car agency office. It took about thirty minutes to get a new car. I helped Jasper move the few items he had in the car to the new vehicle. I didn't say anything other than giving him directions to my house. My stomach tightened as reality was setting in. I wasn't sure he wouldn't turn me in as soon as he knew the truth.

We pulled up to my house. Jasper looked at the place and then at me.

"What is this place?" Jasper asked.

"It's mine."

"Yours?"

"Let's go inside."

"Kathrine?"

"Just come inside, Jasper."

I climbed out of the car and waited for him to follow me. Once Jasper was beside me, I walked him inside. I locked the front door.

"Are we done with the cloak and dagger shit?" Jasper said as he turned around to face me.

"Yes."

"Tell me what the fuck is going on!" Jasper demanded.

I walked up to Jasper and kissed him deeply. If I was going to do this I was going to get one more kiss from him. I wanted to have the memory of the feel of his body and lips. I wanted one more moment of tenderness with him. The kiss lasted only a few minutes. I had my hand on his chest as I stared into his eyes.

"Katherine..."

"My name is Phoenix Redmont not Katherine."

"Phoenix?"

"Yes."

Jasper took a step back from me. I let my hand fall down to my side.

"Why did you give me a fake name?" Jasper placed his hands on his hips as he stood in the middle of the living room.

"Because I was at that party for a specific reason and I never use my real name when I am on a job."

There was a pause in our conversation. I could see the tension in his body the longer this conversation went on.

"What kind of job?"

"I was casing the Augustus house for the painting Love and Pain." I answered.

Jasper was silent for a long time as he stared at me.

"You're a thief?"

"Yes."

I could see his nostrils flaring as he tried to calm himself.

"So what was I to you? Did you plan to use me? What? Get to know me, fuck me, and use me?"

"No. Jasper, I had no clue who you were or that you would even be there." I stepped closer to him.

"Do not touch me!" Jasper stepped away from me.

"Jasper..."

"NO! I do not share anything with anyone but I thought you were different!" Jasper snapped at me.

"Please, let me explain." I pleaded.

"WHY SHOULD I?"

I stood there for a moment seeing the pain he was in.

"I swear I did not know you were going to be there. I had never even heard of you until we met. I had a solid plan until the thief you caught failed to do a job he was forced to. I like you. I had no plan on hurting you or ever involving you in anything but things have changed."

"And I'm supposed to believe you?

"Jasper, please listen to me."

"NO!"

Jasper moved towards the door. I stepped in front of him blocking his path.

"I swear, Jasper. I had no idea who you were before I met you."

"Get out of my way, Phoenix!"

"Not until you listen to what I have to say." I argued.

"I have no desire to waste my time with a liar and a thief."

I stopped moving and stood there. Jasper gave me one final look before he stepped around me. His hand was on the door when I spoke again.

"Silas is the reason we are here." Jasper paused at the door with his hand on the lock.

Jasper finally looked at me. His hand fell away from the door and he turned to face me once more.

"How does Silas fit into this?"

"He set up the theft the other night."

"He was with me when it happened. You were standing right there and saw him. How

could he have any involvement in the attempted theft?"

This was my one chance I would have.

"The man you arrested is known as Gunner in the thief world. He works alone and has a bigger ego than he should but he isn't a guy who steals during events. Gunner prefers more of the after hours work." I explained.

"What does this have to do with Silas?" Jasper questioned me.

"It turns out Gunner was forced to steal from the Augustus house by The Huntsman."

"Who is The Huntsman."

"Silas." I answered.

Jasper stood there a new form of rage filling him. I watched as his eyes shifted to a grey, his wolf peeking through.

"Not possible."

"Silas forced Gunner to try and steal a painting Henry Augustus has in his collection. Gunner failed to retrieve it and Silas ensured he was arrested for his failure."

"How do you know this?"

"Because when I left your room this morning, Silas was waiting in the parking garage for me. He is now forcing me to steal the painting or he will destroy both you and I."

Jasper moved away from the door. I backed away, giving him space.

"No. This is all bullshit."

"Jasper..." I began.

"No! You bring me here, tell me you're an art thief, and I am supposed to just believe you that Silas is a thief who is forcing you to steal a painting?" Jasper snapped at me.

"I know it seems ridiculous but I swear I am telling you the truth."

"Silas is an asshole but he's not a thief. He works for Icarus."

"He was partnered with you because your bosses became suspicious of his behavior."

I could see the gears in his head working.

"Silas had a low rate of retrieval for his client but..."

"He has been a thief for a few years, Jasper. He was using the information he was getting from your company to acquire artwork. That is, until he was partnered with you. After that, he had to stop doing it himself and start forcing others to do it for him."

"How do you know this?" Jasper demanded.

"Because he told me when he cornered me in the parking garage."

"Can you prove any of this?"

"Silas gave me a drive with information about the Augustus house and where the painting is hidden." I showed him the drive.

"How do I know it came from him and you didn't just create all of this to screw with me?"

"I wouldn't do that, Jasper."

"Why, because you care about me?" The bitterness in his voice hurt.

"I know I lied to you but I swear I would never use you or anyone else for my benefit."

Jasper laughed at me.

"You're a thief, Phoenix. It's what you do."

I understood he was hurt but now he was just being a jackass.

"When I steal, it's from people who have millions of dollars. I never engage with other people when I am on a job or grift the owner of the painting. I get in, take what I want, and move on."

"And that's supposed to make me trust you?"

"What do I need to do to prove to you I'm not lying?"

"Nothing. Nothing you can say will change how I feel."

His words cut me deeper than they should.

"I can show you what he gave me and answer any questions you have. I just need you to give me the opportunity." I could see the indecision and anger in his eyes. "Please Jasper, all I'm asking is for you to give me a chance."

"Why did you have lunch with me?"

His question caught me off guard but it meant he was willing to listen to me.

"Because I wanted to. When we met the other night, there was something about you that I liked a lot. I enjoyed our conversation and thought you were attractive. As soon as I found out who you were, I was looking for an escape. Running into you was not part of any plan."

"Why were you there?" Jasper questioned me.

"I was meeting a contact, trying to find out what happened at the party."

Jasper took a step away from the front door, his hands on his hips once more.

"You said when you found out who I was you were looking for an escape."

"Because I do not use others for what I do. It's dirty. As much as I wanted to get to know you, I wasn't willing to take a chance with you." I explained.

His eyes were slowly shifting back to green as his wolf receded.

"Why do you steal art?"

I smiled almost sadly.

"It's a long story."

"If I'm going to trust you, I need you to tell me. I need to know everything."

I nodded understanding him better.

"I'll share my story if you share yours." I countered.

"What?"

"Jasper, you are a wolf who is hiding in plain sight of humans. You are the best Icarus has ever had as an investigator. If you expect me to share pieces of my life with you, you have to do the same."

"Phoenix..."

"You want to trust me so you are asking me about who I am. This goes both ways."

Jasper sighed.

"It's not the same thing. I'm not hurting anyone." Jasper argued.

"You're not? How many of the humans you work with would feel that way if they learned what you are? They wouldn't feel betrayed? Besides, none of the people I steal from ever meet me. I do not ransack anyone's home or go after random items. I take art from rich people who have it because they have the money to buy it."

"You don't think those people aren't hurt by your actions?"

"The one who takes a hit is companies like Icarus. Jasper and I were silent. "Look, we do not have to agree about this. We both break rules to get what we want. Can we just sit down and be open with one another?"

"Okay."

Jasper took a seat on the sofa and I followed his lead.

"You really want to know my story?"

"If I'm going to tell you mine, I need you to put the same trust in me with your story." I replied.

"I needed a job when I turned eighteen. My parents are not much of the parental figure types and I had to support myself. As I moved up the lie just continued. I built my career on the lie that I was human. The way I saw it, the situation was that I was proving how I and all other hellborns are better than the humans were. Every time I show them up, it's a win." Jasper explained.

I understood that all too well.

"Thank you for telling me." I took a breath before I started. "I started stealing because I needed to find a way to survive. I lost the only family I had when I was sixteen. I didn't have any desire to be in foster care so the little money my mother left me I lived off of. I knew it wouldn't be enough to survive so I got a job but it didn't pay enough. I began to steal to ensure I was okay. One day, I wandered into a museum and found that art was something I truly could love. I started to steal for more than survival. I was stealing for the love of art. The pieces I have less love for provide for my lifestyle. The pieces that move my soul, I keep."

Jasper smiled at me.

"I get the love you have for art."

"Do you?"

"Yes." We sat in silence for a minute. "We are both liars for our own benefit. I guess you were right. We are more alike than I believed."

"I knew we were when I researched you and during our lunch." I smiled.

Jasper nodded his head.

"What is Silas threatening you with?"

"To expose you and to throw me in jail if I don't do what he wants. To add to my misery, he is also threatening to take my entire collection and sell it off one piece at a time." I explained.

I could see the anger in his face.

"What does he want exactly?"

"He wants a painting that hasn't been seen since World War II. It was believed that the Nazis destroyed it."

"What's the name of the paint?" Jasper's face looked confused.

"Portrait of a Young Boy."

"I know Augustus' collection. I was the one who had it cataloged and appraised. He doesn't have any painting that is a lost piece of artwork."

"I know what Icarus has listed for his art collection but that doesn't mean he doesn't have it."

"Are sure Augustus has this painting?" Jasper asked.

"I don't know. Silas seems sure about it and if he does he has it hidden somewhere."

"It could be anywhere, Phoenix."

I smiled at Jasper. I liked hearing him say my name.

"It will be in the most secure part of the house."

"I have seen his entire art room. That painting isn't there." Jasper assured me.

"If Augustus was found to have a painting that was believed to have been stolen and destroyed by the Nazis, it would require him to answer where he got the piece. Correct?"

"Yes. It would be invaluable and every museum would want it. We would have to authenticate the piece which would take weeks and ensure that he upped his security measures."

"If he has it and is hiding it, it means he probably obtained it either illegally." I replied.

"Which would lead to his insurance company investigating every painting he owns."

"Which could lead to other investigations in his life."

"Let's see what Silas gave you."

Chapter Ten

It took a few minutes for me to get the computer up and running. I kept the Wifi router off. Jasper and I plugged the thumb drive into my computer. Before I opened any of the files, I began a scan on it. Call it paranoia but I wasn't taking the chance that The Huntsman didn't place a worm inside of one of the files. I had one of the best programs for tracking unwanted software. It took several minutes for the scan to finish and inform me that the drive was clean. Jasper and I said nothing to one another as we waited. We sat on my sofa side by side. I wanted to believe that this could be the start of something between us but I was leery of the feelings. How could we make this work? Or was I kidding myself? Of course there was the chance that once we caught The Huntsman, Jasper could arrest both of us? There were too many what ifs for me to process right at that moment. I pushed the thoughts away and focused on the computer.

There were a total of three files on the device. The first was an image of the painting, dimensions and its history. It was a small Neoclassical painting created by Raphael. He had painted it on a thin canvas cloth, making it easier to hide. It had been stolen in Poland in the mid 1940s. At the time of its disappearance, Nazis were raiding museums and jewish homes, taking artwork for Hilter. These pieces were placed in caves, warehouses, and anywhere they could hide them from public view. Eventually, the Allies began to hunt the artwork. Some were recovered but there was also a large portion that were destroyed to keep them from being returned. Portrait of a Young Man was a painting whose whereabouts had been missing since the war. According to the file, Henry Augustus obtained the painting three years ago from an art dealer in Louisiana. The art dealer in question was known for purchasing items off the black market. There had been investigations into the dealer but nothing ever came of them.

The next file was information about the house, security system, the security company Henry Augustus was using. He had even included a few of the passwords into the system. It was all of the information I would need.

The last file was actual images of the art room. The files showed me exactly who The Huntsman was as a thief. I was not a thief that needed to write all of this information down. I memorized what I needed to know. I studied plans and what I could gather about the security system. I made several versions of plans so that I had several escape routes, ways to get to the artwork, and how I could hide. Other thieves like The Huntsman felt the need to write everything down. They had less confidence in their skills. They needed notes to create a plan for themselves. I was guessing prior to working at Icarus. He was a small-time thief, taking pieces that few truly cared about. He needed the advantage that Icarus could give him.

"Are we sure Augustus has this painting?" Jasper asked as soon as saw the painting.

I looked at him.

"From the information Silas has given us, I believe so."

"How can we be sure he's telling the truth?" I looked at Jasper. "Look, I have seen every painting in that art room. We know Silas is threatening to ruin both of us. He has already destroyed one thief's life. How do we know this isn't all a lie?"

I smiled at him.

"You're so cute." I said as I went back to the photos of the art room.

"What?"

"You're thinking like an investigator not like an art thief."

"I spend my days thinking like an art thief. It's why I'm good at what I do."

"No, you think like a very basic art thief, not like I do. Augustus is like a sophisticated art thief." I turned to face Jasper. "This particular painting would be worth probably more than his entire collection. As soon as he obtained the painting, he knew he had to hide it away so know one would know about it."

"Why have it then?"

Owning a painting like this gives him a satisfaction that nothing else can give him. I would say Augustus is hiding it in a room you are unaware of or within that art room. It could be in a painting or a hidden wall safe or even in a room connected to the art room that you have no clue about. From everything we have here plus what I learned on my own about Henry, he probably has a secret room or it has been tucked away inside another painting. Most thieves do not like having their loot far from them." I explained.

Jasper was studying me.

"What about you?"

"What about me?"

"Do you keep your paintings here?" Jasper was looking at the living room.

"I like you Jasper, I could even love you, but for you to know where I keep my artwork, I have to know you have no plans on arresting me or taking what is mine. The only way for us to get to that point is for us to spend a lot of time together and even then I will have a hard time sharing that information."

Jasper gave me a smirk.

"What if I promise I will not arrest you?"

"Trust is built Jasper, not just given blindly." I gave him a soft kiss before I turned back to the computer.

I began to examine the photos of the art room. I read through The Huntsman's notes. He had studied the room and found nothing odd about it. There were several paintings within the collection that looked to have been taken apart. According to the records Icarus obtained, Mr.

Augustus had had those paintings clean. The Huntsman believed that somewhere within that room the painting was tucked away. I opened the other file, comparing the photos to the blueprints.

"If Silas is correct, the piece is hidden behind the painting that hangs here." I used the mouse cursor to point to the painting.

"Love and Dread would be a good option or the one at the other end of the room Gather Ye Rosebuds." I wanted to curse. "The first painting is a..."

"I know the painting." I answered.

"Of course you do." Jasper taunted me with a smile.

I gave the wolf a look. If I was as unlucky as I was feeling right now, the painting was going to be inside of Love and Dread.

"Have you seen the wall behind these paintings?" I asked.

"Yes."

"Is there any seam in the wall that shouldn't be there?"

"No."

"Does the room feel off, like it's smaller than it should be?" I asked.

"No."

I sat looking at the images and flipped back to the blueprints The Huntsman gave me. They indicated that the wall aligned with the wall on the floor above.

"Did you pull the blueprints of the house?"

"No. We look at the security system they use, then have a curator come in and verify the pieces within the room. If there needs to be any adjustments to how the art is protected we inform them of what the client needs to do."

I took in what Jasper said. I flipped back to the images and examined each one, zooming in and looking at the wall panels. I looked at the information about The Portrait of a Young Man and read the dimensions. I studied the images of the room and questioned if Silas had the correct blueprints. I read more of Silas' notes seeing he believed there was a hidden spot in the wall or a secret room. The basement was off in terms of dimensions but only by a few inches. That could be easily explained. He would have put in place a special air filter which would mean the walls need to come in to make room for it.

I looked at the two other hiding places. If there was a fire within the house Henry would want his priceless possession hidden close to an exit. He would also pick the piece that was less desired by most collectors. Love and Dread was less desired and was closest to the exit.

"I need the blueprints from city hall to confirm but I'm confident that he's wrong where it is hidden."

"What do you mean?"

"Silas believes the painting is behind this wall but it's not. It's in the canvas of Love and Dread." I explained.

Jasper said nothing as he studied the images.

"How do you know for sure?"

"I don't. The only way I will know is for me to eliminate a secret room from the equation. Getting the blueprints will tell me everything that The Huntsman gave me the correct information and ..."

"To get into the room to eliminate his theory or pry the back off of Love and Pain."

"Yes. If the secret room doesn't exist, I'll have to pry Love and Pain's wood away from the canvas."

"There is risk though. Prying open the back of a painting could damage the wood on the back or even the canvas." Jasper pointed out.

"If you know what you are doing all it takes is a few tools and time. The painting will not be harmed." I said with a smile. Jasper looked at me almost impressed. "What?"

"You are an interesting female."

"Why do you say that?"

"I have interviewed a lot of thieves over the years. I have held conversations with them. None of them had the excitement as you do about the actual artwork."

"Most thieves steal for money or glory. I don't because you'll never be rich from stealing art and there is something about the entire thing that bothers me. There are places we can sell the art we steal and make good money. There are auctions in the underworld where people like Augustus go for their pieces. Fake documents are easily given so it appears to be a legal sale. It all seems dirty and it always has to me. I hate selling the art I steal but do it when I need to. I see how an artist uses certain brush strokes to create emotions in those that see their work. I see how much effort it requires to create a piece like Love and Dread. Art is supposed to be studied, observed, and loved. It's not for bragging rights or to be hidden from others to see. Guys like Henry Augustus buy art so that they can say they have it," I explained.

"You truly love the art you steal?"

"Yes."

An understanding passed between us as we sat on my couch.

"Should we start planning our heist?" Jasper asked.

"Our heist?"

"You brought me in on this."

"I know but..."

"I will not allow you to do this yourself."

"Jasper..." I took a breath. "I brought you in to take down Silas. I will get the painting but you will need to get him. I do not want you to be part of the stealing."

"I can't just allow you to put yourself on the line." Jasper reached over and placed a hand on my cheek.

I gave him a sad smile. His need to be part of every inch of this made me love him. I also knew what it would mean for him to do this.

"If you do this, you will not be able to go back." I pointed out.

"I know. I also know I cannot prove who Silas truly is unless I help you. The other thief is refusing to talk to anyone. These documents you have could have come from anywhere. I have no proof he is part of this other than your word which gets us nowhere legally."

He was right but I didn't like it.

"I can do this without you." I offered.

"No."

"This is what I do. It's who I am. You are the guy I run from and if you do this it will mean your life gets turned upside down and I don't want that. All I want is to stop Silas."

He leaned forward and kissed me quickly.

"My life was already turned upside down as soon as I met you. What kind of male would I be if I allowed you to face this without me?"

"The kind that doesn't deserve this."

"I am not a male that walks away when things get hard." Jasper argued. "Now, how do we pull this off?"

I didn't know how to argue with him but I wanted to. I didn't want this to destroy Jasper and everything he built for himself. I also knew that no matter what I said Jasper would not be swayed.

"Not much, just a few things."

Chapter Eleven

I memorized the house plans quickly and shut down the computer. I placed the device in its hidden compartment and sat back down on the sofa.

"Most of what we need I already have. The tools needed to get the painting I have. A few small screwdrivers, lock picking kit, a laser pointer for the cameras, and a pocketknife should be all I need."

"What about getting it out of the house or even us getting inside?" Jasper asked.

I smiled.

"That part is more tricky particularly with there being two of us."

"Why do you say that?"

"Usually when I do a job I have a way already in a party or a city worker. I have set up my way in well prior to the job. I don't have that luxury this time." I explained.

"Okay, what is the other issue?"

"My escape routes generally only have to be good enough for me to get out. Planning a two man entry and exit can get more complicated."

"How many days did Silas give you to retrieve the painting?" Jasper asked.

"A week."

"Any other issues?"

"We have no idea what condition the painting is in which could make things difficult to move it. Best case it's in great condition which means I can get it out by slipping it into something to transport it or on my body."

"And worst case?"

"Even touching the painting will harm it. There is also the issue with your presence at work. You should be heading back to New York with Silas. In order for us to pull this off together, I need you here. From everything I have learned about you, you're not a male who misses work. If you call out now Silas will get suspicious."

"Okay. I could head back to New York while you get things we need. As soon as I arrive I can give my final report and put in for a vacation time."

"It's an idea but Silas could still question your actions."

"Not if I take two weeks off. I can make it look like I just need some time to recover from all of the traveling I've been doing for work. It will take me a couple days but I could be back here in two or three days."

"Okay that would solve that issue. Now I just need to find a way for us to get into the house."

"What if I tell Augustus that I want to do another check of his property for security purposes?"

"It could work but what if he calls Icarus to check. If that happens it will tip off Silas that something isn't right."

We sat in silence for a moment.

"Henry was upset that he wasn't allowed to have any more events for the next three months. What if I lift the restriction?"

"You would need a reason to?"

"I could require him to add two more guards to the property and close off part of the house to ensure that no one can have access to the art room."

"It could work."

"I could find out what measures he will take in order to meet the new security measures."

"What if he doesn't?"

"He will. Henry likes to party too much not to agree to my terms."

I thought it through if it worked, we could be inside by the end of the week. If it failed I would have to do it the old school way of your standard breaking and entering. I hated doing them because they had no sophistication to them. There was a high risk to them as well.

"When do you leave?" I asked.

"Tonight." Jasper's phone rang, startling both of us. He looked at his phone. "It's Silas."

"Don't answer it. He could track you."

Jasper let the phone ring until it went to voicemail.

"I should go before he calls again."

Jasper stood up and walked to the door. I followed behind him.

"Be safe and don't call him back until you are at least ten miles from here."

I stood in front of him. Jasper grabbed me by the waist and pulled me to him. He kissed me, making me catch my breath.

"As soon as I land I will call you."

That made me think of a new problem.

"Hold that thought."

I ran to my spare bedroom. It took me a few minutes to get into my hidden safe. I pulled out a prepaid phone. It was a spare that I kept in case of emergencies. I ran back into the living room.

"Only use this to call me. It can't be traced and will not lead you back to me if something happens."

Jasper took the phone and slid it into the pocket of his jeans. He gave me one more kiss before he left. I watched as he pulled away from my home, already missing him more than I should. I turned away from the window and went to work. I needed to figure out all the potential pitfalls of our current plan and make sure we had everything we needed.

Chapter Twelve

Jasper arrived in New York later that evening. I stayed awake waiting to hear from him. He sent me a message informing me he was home. I hated the thought that he would have to sit on a plane next to Silas and pretend nothing was wrong. It would take him at most two days to get everything in place on his end. It also led me to question what I was doing with Jasper. Yes, both of our lives were on the line but it didn't mean I was right for being honest with Jasper. It didn't make it right that I brought him into my world. There was a part of me that questioned if I should go without him. I could get the painting using the most basic techniques. It placed me in danger of being caught but it also saved Jasper potentially. The thoughts kept me up longer than I should have been.

The next day there was radio silence between Jasper and I which I tried to ignore. I focused on what I needed to do.

The first piece I thought about was the painting itself and how to get it out of the house. My best option was to plan for the painting to be in terrible condition. It meant I couldn't roll the canvas up or hide it in a bag or in a tool box. I would need to keep the painting flat and that limited my options. The only way to do that was to attach it to my body. I would need K-tape, cotton cloth, and cotton inspection gloves. I would place the painting between two pieces of cloth and tape it to my body. The K-Tape would ensure I could get the material off my body easily.

The easiest part of the heist was getting the artwork out. The real task was now to figure out how I was getting it. Silas' notes gave me a more detailed idea of what I was up against. Jasper would fill in the gaps of any changes that were being made. The problem was getting into the house without too much detection. We were hoping Henry Augustus was going to take the bait and throw a party. If he did, I could ensure I ended up on the guest list. There were a few problems that could arise. The first was what if Icarus refused the upgrades he would need. It would mean any party he had was delayed. I had a matter of days not weeks to get the painting. There was also the possibility that Henry would reject Jasper's recommendations. Henry was a man that didn't like being told. He could say no to Icarus and there was no party at all.

This led me to my second option. I could pretend to be a city employee and use a ruse to get into the house. I could be a city inspector who needs to check the house for whatever reason. It would be easy enough to enter the house in this way but getting left alone would mean I need diversion. There were risks in doing things this way. What if the diversion doesn't work? Or if it's not a big enough diversion. The Augustus family had a crappy security team but it was still a security team. They also had at least three people on staff that could pose a problem. All it takes is one slip up or missing one person and I was caught.

The last option was a simple breaking and entering. It was a risk I didn't like. I could go in during the dead of night. An all-night shift would probably ensure there were no security guards, only a system. I could bypass the system and at least for a few minutes. I would have to work quickly and pray I was correct in where the painting was. If I was wrong, I would have to make my escape without the painting or attempt to get into the other painting. Either way, it created issues for me to make a clean break. My main goal on any job was ensure I was never seen or any trace of me was left behind. Option two and three had too many variables to ensure success. The first option was going to be my best choice. I would have to wait to see if Augustus took the bait.

I made plans for all three options, trying to have multiple escape routes for each one. All of the plans I created kept Jasper on the outside of the house while I did the dirty work. If I failed, the only one who would get arrested was me. It wouldn't prevent Silas from destroying Jasper's career but it ensured he could still work towards taking The Huntsman down.

The next part of my planning was to ensure Jasper had what he needed to catch Silas. I set up two safety deposit boxes in different aliases at two different banks with him as the beneficiary. I made copies of the information Silas gave me, placing a copy in each one.

By the end of the day, I was making sleep potions. The potions would be my last-ditch efforts to save myself. I already had a few made but I still worked in my kitchen to make new ones. When a sleeping potion weren't enough to distract me, I switched gears and moved to making a few other potions. One was for coating scents and another for disorientation. Both would help but were not really necessary. If I needed those two spells I would be in trouble.

I finished my spell making only to find myself not being able to sit still. I went back to my plans and began to analyze each one. I worked through all of the holes I had, every potential pitfall. Each plan had its potential to fail, some just had more than others. I began to pace the living room. When I couldn't pace any longer, I began to pull my tools out. I checked the laser to ensure it was functioning at its full capacity. I made sure my lock picking tools were together. I even double checked and cleaned my screwdrivers. I didn't want to take any chances of leaving any traces of wood or anything else behind. I checked my inspection gloves and decided I needed to get a new pair. I had used them for a few jobs which would mean fibers were present. I pulled a sealed pair of gloves from my supply stash and added them to my tools.

After doing all of that I was only in the early hours of the evening. It had been almost a full twenty-four hours since I had heard from Jasper. It had been part of our plan to keep quiet but it didn't mean I liked it. Not knowing what was happening was creating more anxiety. It made me want to just go for the breaking and entering plan. If I just made my move I could have it within hours. From there I could create a plan to set The Huntsman up to take the fall. The problem was there was no way to do that without taking myself out. I didn't want to end up in jail for years to come. I knew all too well how one count could turn into several counts. Waiting a few days was still the best option.

I had a feeling it was going to be a long night with little sleep.

Chapter Thirteen

I spent the majority of my night trying to relax and failing. I cleaned my tools several times, I made sure that I wore gloves to ensure if I lost one no fingerprints or trace evidence would be found on any of them. I tried to watch a movie only to find myself distracted. I stopped the movie several times to just pace as my brain tried to find another plan, one that made me feel better about the entire situation. The issue was there wasn't any other plan.

I eventually fell asleep on my sofa as I watched television until I woke in the early hours of the morning to knocking on my door. I sat up and waited as the knocking stopped and waited. A moment later the knocking started once more. I crossed the room quietly and looked out the peephole. Standing at my door was Jasper. I threw the door open and took in all of him.

"I couldn't wait another day and not know if you were safe."

"You idiot." I said as I pulled him inside.

We stood in my living room, kissing one another.

I kissed Jasper like my life depended on it. He responded by wrapping his arms around me, pulling me as close to him. The kiss lasted only a moment more before I pulled my lips from his. I stepped out of his arms and grabbed his hand, leading him to my bedroom. I had never allowed any male into my home. Any time I spent a night with a male was at their place or a hotel room. I wanted Jasper in my bed. I wanted his scent on my sheets. I wanted him.

I pulled his shirt off of him, taking in his beautiful body. I placed a hand on his chest as I moved close to him. His hands moved under my night shirt, touching my bare skin for a split second. He pulled my shirt off me as his hands ran down my back down to my ass, his lips claiming mine. We kissed one another harshly as his hands memorized the curves of my body. The feel of his hands on me were enough to make my body tighten.

Jasper was the one to end our kiss this time.

"Lay down, Phoenix." Jasper ordered me.

I gave him a wicked smile as I slid onto the bed. I moved into the center of it. My eyes on him as I moved. Jasper watched me, his eyes were bright green now. I watched as he slowly undid his jeans and stripped out of them. He stood at the edge of my bed for a moment, his long thick cock hard and gorgeous. Jasper climbed slowly onto the bed placing himself above me. I spread my legs for him, feeling his dick pressed against me. Jasper kissed me slowly as he entered me. The feeling took me by surprise, causing me to gasp. Jasper pulled his lips away from mine. He watched my face as his hips moved in a slow rhythm. He entered me, going deeper with each stroke until he was buried deep inside of me. I came around him with his name on my lips. I moved my hips meeting his movement as the waves of my orgasm continued. The feel of his body pressed against me with his dick deep inside of me was better than any heist I had ever pulled off.

I felt as Jasper's movement changed as he moved faster. I could feel the tension in his body. He sat up on his knees not missing a stroke as his hands grabbed my hips. He moved his hips more aggressively, hitting that spot with every move. I dug my hands into the mattress as his love making moved into undeniable need. I watched Jasper as he watched our bodies come together. A growl slipped from his lips as he moved faster. My body responding to the feel of his desire, coming over and over again. I felt as Jasper finally allowed himself to come deep inside of me. His head fell back onto his shoulders. We were both panting as he looked down at me. His wolf was in his eyes.

"Jasper." I said softly as I reached up to touch his body.

"I'm not done with you."

His words made my body become wet again.

He pulled out of me and flipped me over. I arched my back as he placed himself behind me. He entered me harshly with his hand sliding into my hair as he fucked me. His other hand gripped my shoulder. He slammed into me making me cry out as I orgasmed hard around him. He didn't stop, just kept going. I was lost in the feeling of him and the claiming that was happening.

Jasper released my hair and wrapped his arm around my body pulling me up against him. He sat back on his knees.

"You are mine, Phoenix. Mine!" Jasper growled into my ear, his hand around the base of my throat.

His words were a whole new high for me.

"My wolf."

My words sent a new charge through both of us. Everything slipped away as he showed me who I belonged to. It was earth shattering. I would never be the same after this.

Chapter Fourteen

Jasper and I lay in bed with me on his chest and his arm draped around me.

"How did you get here?" I asked.

"I drove my car down and parked it a few miles out. I transformed as soon as I was in the trees and ran until I found your scent."

"And your clothes?"

"Like any other good wolf, I tied them to me."

I pictured my wolf running through the trees with clothes tied to his body. We lay in bed for a while longer until I broke the silence again.

"You weren't supposed to be here for another day."

"I couldn't wait. I needed to be here with you."

I looked up at Jasper.

"I felt the same way but what if..." my voice died.

"What?"

"What if Silas realizes what we are doing? It's why you were supposed to wait before you came back."

"He won't."

I sat up a little so I could look at him.

"Thieves live in a state of what ifs and looking at every possible reason a plan could fail. I can guarantee that he has considered the possibility that you know what is happening."

"I made sure I complained about how exhausted I am and how I needed a long vacation most of the flight. I even went as far as snapping at Silas a few times, which I enjoyed more than I should have. Before I even landed, I called our supervisors saying that I needed a break after so many trips. I even made sure he saw that I was purchasing a ticket to Montana."

Jasper had done everything he could to throw Silas off his trail.

"What about Henry Augustus?"

"He has been given the option of resuming his parties as long as he adds two guards to the property."

"Anything else?"

"He is adding two cameras at the door to the art room."

"Okay." I began to think through the new information.

"Do you know where the guards will be posted?"

"Yes, I do." There was hesitation in his voice.

"Where?"

"Two will be at the entrance of the property ensuring no one brings anything questionable inside, another outside the art room. The rest will be with part goers."

"Metal detectors?" I asked.

"No."

"That's an upside. Any idea of when his next party is?"

"None."

The wheels in my head began to turn. Henry Augustus liked flashy events. He wouldn't wait long to have a party but would it be soon enough? I would need two plans.

"What are you thinking?"

"I need to have two plans." I answered.

"You mean we."

"If he throws a party, it will be both of us going in. If he doesn't, I'll need you waiting for me."

"What do you mean?" Jasper asked.

"I mean you will have to be my getaway driver."

Jasper rolled on his side resting his head on his fist.

"I don't like the idea of you going in there alone."

"I know but it minimizes the chances of getting caught and ensures you are safe."

"Don't worry about me."

"I have to worry about you, Jasper." I replied.

"No, you don't."

"Jasper..."

"I'm in this and I'm not walking away." Jasper said.

He kissed me, giving me only his lips. When I started this my biggest fear was losing my freedom and my art. Now it was the thought of losing him.

Chapter Fifteen

Jasper and I spent the entire day in bed with one another. It was in some ways a waste of the short time we had left but it was time that I would never get back. The next day I began to work on both plans. The breaking and entering would be easy enough. The windows were going to be the entry point, particularly the windows on the west side of the house. It was on the same side as the pool house. Augustus' son came and left at all hours of the day and the night. Meaning that Henry did little to keep that side of the house secured. It also gave me a story if I was caught. I would enter with my tools attached to my body. I would disable the cameras with my laser and enter the art room. I would have roughly five minutes or less to get the painting and get out. I would meet Jasper on the next block exiting from the back of the property.

Plan B was the plan I liked best. Jasper and I would enter Henry Augustus' party together as a couple. I would ensure we arrived when the majority of the guests were also arriving because it would make the security guards sloppy. They would feel the pressure of getting people inside meaning they would not do a secure check of my bag. It would be a simple in and out job with no one knowing what we were doing until we were already gone. I began to put together the breaking and entering kit I would need while Jasper kept a close eye on everything Henryand his wife posted on social media.

Within two days, an invitation had arrived for a party at Henry Augustus in one of my emails. The party would take place at the end of the week. They were having another masquerade party. It created a perfect opportunity for Jasper and I to get to the painting.

The first step was ensuring Jasper would not be recognized. Being that the party would be a masquerade would help cover his identity. It took me several hours to create a new name and identification for him. I made sure I built him a LinkedIn account placing him within the hierarchy of my made up wine company. He was given the vice president role. There was no photo of him to ensure no one used software recognition or noticed him. By the time I was done, he had a new name, job, and identity online.

Once that was done, I took him shopping for a new mask and to get a new outfit for me. I found a black halter style cocktail dress that was short and loose on the bottom. I found a new red velvet cap and a silver and black mask with a soft fleur-de-lis design along the edges to complete the outfit. Jasper's mask was a silver and black wolf. The mask covered most of his face which would make it easy for him to move through the party unnoticed. I found a silver and black tie that would complete his look. He would be my Big Bad Wolf and I his Red Riding Hood. Jasper enjoyed the irony of the costumes I picked for us.

We would arrive at the party when it was already in full swing. My plan was to go through security when they were the busiest. It would allow me to hide my tools in plain sight and ensure security wouldn't be paying close enough attention. Once inside, we would move through the party as I had done before, waiting for party goers to get a few drinks deep and for security to relax into their roles of monitoring the party goers.

At some point, we would make our way into the house. I would use a potion to dose the security officer on duty outside of the art gallery while Jasper would shut down the video feed. Jasper would create a loop that made it appear everything was safe and secure. They would see the security guard standing guard and no one in the hall. As a male who worked to catch thieves, he understood how to use a security system to our advantage. As soon as I knew it was safe to enter the art room, I would go in and find the painting. It would give me at most fifteen minutes to find it. In truth, it would be more like a six-to-eight-minute window. Once I had the painting, I would make my escape and we would leave with no one the wiser.

I would contact The Huntsman and set up a meeting as soon as we were out of the house. That was when we would get him. I would meet him alone with one of my phones recording our meeting. It was then my job to get him to admit what he had done while Jasper listened in. Jasper would use the information to not only secure me a deal but also take Silas down. Once The Huntsman was in custody, Jasper would take the painting and open an investigation on Augustus and how he obtained the other painting. I would lose my opportunity to have Love and Dread but it would ensure Jasper was protected and I didn't go to jail. I would go into hiding after that for several months. It would also mean more than likely Jasper and I would not be able to speak for a while. Jasper would close out the case on Silas and Henry Augustus and walk away from Icarus. He would meet up with me and we would decide together what was next for us.

I had spent most of my life alone and loving it. I lived my life the way I wanted and didn't concern myself with anyone. I hid among society. The days Jasper and I spent together felt natural. It was a feeling I never had before and one that scared the hell out of me. We moved in a room perfectly with one another with little thought. We spent time talking about everything from politics, to world events, art work, and our lives. We cleaned and cooked side by side. We slept in my bed every night curled up beside one another and woke up together. I could see the life we could live together.

As the days ticked by and we got closer to the party another reality set in deep inside of me. I wanted a life with Jasper but I was never going to be a law abiding citizen. I lived a life as a nomad with several names in different locations. Could I walk away from being an art thief? I wanted to think I could but what did I do? Get a nine to five? The thought made me sick to my stomach. Jasper was not that male.

He deserved more than I could give him. He deserved a female who followed the law, who could give him a family, someone who didn't bounce around the country stealing art. I didn't want to lose my wolf but I also wanted him to have a life that was better than me.

The day of the heist I woke up curled against Jasper, one arm wrapped around me the other under my pillow. I took in the feel of his body against mine, memorizing the feel of him. I wanted more time with him. I wanted to have more mornings like this but I knew after today this was over. It would have to be. We both had the plan that we would build a life with one another but I was losing faith in that part of the plan. He would get The Huntsman and I would go into hiding. We would never have an option for happily ever after. That thought broke a piece of me.

"Are you nervous?" Jasper asked quietly.

I rolled over and looked at him.

"No. Are you?"

"A little."

I placed my hands on my face and gave him a quick kiss.

"You could always wait in the car for me and I could do this myself."

"No."

"Jasper, you could lose everything if we are caught. For me, this is just part of my life, part of what I do. Let me do this for both of us."

"My life is already forever altered because of you. I will not allow you to place yourself in harm's way to protect me."

"I need to apologize for that first part."

"That's…"

The alarm went off. I rolled away from him and turned it off before he could say the words, I knew he wanted to say.

"We should make sure we have everything we need for tonight."

I climbed out of bed and headed out into the living room. I couldn't let him finish his sentence. Hearing how he felt about me would make it so much more difficult to walk away from him.

WE SPENT THE HOURS leading up to the party ensuring we had everything we would need. The purse I was carrying was slightly bigger than I normally would take to an event like this. It looked like a basket with a red cotton lining. I split the lining, placing a pocketknife inside the lining dumping my screwdriver. I placed a lipstick, a compact and a few feminine products inside. The one thing I have learned as a thief is that men and males all operate the same way when it comes to certain products. They would see the products and only that when they looked in my purse and would push me through.

The purse also served to help get the painting out of the house. I had two options: either roll the painting up in my purse or on my body using k-tape. I placed some k-tape inside my purse as well. I would enter the party with some on my shoulder as a cover that I was injured in a small wreck. If asked, the tape was to give me support for a bad shoulder. I lined the purse with two small pieces of clothes. If I went with the second option, the cloth would protect the painting. The last item I placed in my purse was a small perfume bottle. The scent was flowery but if sprayed would drop any hellborn or human for several hours. It was my way of using potions. I hid a small lock picking set in my bra. As far as we were aware they were only checking bags making it easy to slip the kit in.

Once I made sure I had everything we would need, I had Jasper log into the Augustus' security system. He took the extra step creating a back door within the system, making our job easier once we were inside. His training he had been given with Icarus had prepared him for this robbery in more than one way. I added a small laser I had made a few upgrades on in case we needed to use them on one of the other cameras.

By seven thirty we were leaving the house and heading to the Augustus' masquerade ball. According to the invitation, the festivities began at seven. By the time we arrived it would be eight p.m., which ensured that there would be a long line of guests waiting to enter. Their desire to get inside would create an issue for security. Inside the party, the drinks would be flowing. With any luck, most would be on their second or third drink by the time we walked in. The more people at the party drank the more difficult it would be for anyone to remember too many details.

The drive as before took thirty minutes. We parked down the street and sat for a moment. Normally at this point of the job I was calm, reviewing my moves in my head as I entered into the property. This was different. The adrenaline was starting to flow through my body meaning it could cause problems during the job.

"Are you ready for your first heist?" I asked Jasper as we watched partygoers arrive.

"It's what Icarus trained me for."

I laughed at him.

"Not sure that this was part of their plans for you."

"Maybe not, but here we are." Jasper leaned towards me. He brought my face towards his and kissed me. I wanted another day with him but I also knew that wasn't possible. I ended our kiss before I was ready.

"Shall we?" I asked.

"Yes."

We pulled on our masks and stepped out of the car. I walked around the front of the car as Jasper reached his hand out to me. We walked to the house saying nothing. People were filing into the mansion slowly. To my surprise there was no one checking bags as there was supposed to be. A part of me was grateful for Augustus' arrogance.

The other part made me wonder what other changes we were not aware of.

As before, the party was like any other rich man's party. The music was boring, trays of small finger foods were being served. People talked among each other with drinks in their hands. As I predicted, people were already well on their way to being drunk. Jasper and I found a small table to stand at so it appeared we were deep in conversation. He placed himself where he was pressed close to me, a hand around my waist as he leaned his head down. I felt as he took a deep breath, trying to slow the flow of adrenaline.

"I didn't get a chance to tell you how beautiful you look tonight." Jasper said.

I looked up at him, seeing his desire for me. I gave him a quick kiss on the lips before I responded.

"You look quite dashing yourself."

"What can I say, I clean up well." Jasper gave me a grin.

I giggled at him. People mingled around us, the volume growing slowly as more people arrived.

As before, Augustus came out and made a speech about how he was so happy everyone could attend. The difference this time was that he clapped his hands twice at the end and performers came out of the pool house. The performers were dressed as circus performers as they began to do tumbles. A fire breather was balancing on one of the rails as she blew a flame at the crowd. The guests were distracted, it was the perfect time to move into the house.

"Escort me to the bathroom, my wolf." I suggested.

"As you wish, Red."

We moved through the crowd as everyone watched the performances. There were people in the house talking with one another. I glanced around the area ensuring no one was paying us any attention. Jasper kept his hand on the small of my back as we moved through the house. I found the bathroom that was down the hall from the art room. We stopped outside it. Jasper placed his back against the wall as I positioned myself in front of him. I pressed my body against him as he pulled the burner phone from his pocket. He accessed the security system from the phone. It took Jasper a few minutes to do his part. I kissed his neck and cheek as I waited. He looked at me for a moment and kissed me giving me just his lips.

"There are two security guards outside the art gallery. One on each side of the hall."

"Follow my lead. Once they are down, ensure no one comes this way."

"Will do. The loop is up." Jasper whispered.

Before we moved I looked at Jasper.

"If I'm not out of the gallery in ten minutes leave without me."

"Not happening."

"Jasper..."

"No. We are in this together."

I didn't have time to argue with him. I gave him a look and headed down the hall with Jasper at my back. We turned the corner to see two security guards standing at the end of the hall. I turned to Jasper and smiled.

"What did I tell you?" Jasper gave me a look unsure what I was doing. "We should have never come to this party tonight."

I smacked his chest.

"You said you wanted to go out more." Jasper's voice was harsh.

"Hey this area is off-limits." One of the security guards spoke to us. They both moved down the hall towards us.

I pulled the perfume bottle from my purse.

"You call this going out. I wanted to dance and have a few drinks. This is some stuck up, boring ass party."

"Hey!" The security guards were almost to us.

"You are so damn needy!" Jasper snapped at me.

I turned to the security officer and sprayed the first one in the face. Within seconds he hit the floor. The second guard watched as his buddy collapsed. I sprayed him as he looked back at us and he hit the floor as well. I stepped over them.

Jasper smiled at me as he reached into his inside breast pocket and pulled a laser pointer from his pocket. The security loop would only work for the first five to ten minutes at most. The laser would damage the camera which ensured it picked up nothing else. He held the laser in his hand as he placed himself against the wall.

"Go Red."

I smiled and headed to the art room. I walked inside the room seeing the walls were painted dark blue. The lights were soft with smaller lights over each painting. Love and Dread sat in the middle of the wall on the right side. He had changed the order of the paintings. I didn't delay as I moved. I ran my hand along the wall to ensure I was correct. I looked at the dimensions of the room. I didn't find any hidden seams or anything that was off enough for me to believe the painting was behind the wall.

I reached the painting. I took a moment to take in the beauty of it wishing I could have it. The brush strokes were smooth and even. Her hair was a stunning red that most couldn't create as Edvard Munch had. The pain the male was in was so clear as his love held him. The need to take it was rooted deep in me. I couldn't have it, not now, probably not ever after all of this.

I had a job to do. I pulled on a pair of gloves. I lifted the painting off the wall and placed it on the floor. I kneeled down as I looked at the back. I pulled the pocketknife from my purse. There were three pieces of wood that were being used as braces on the back of the painting. The three pieces I needed to loosen were being held in place by screws that didn't match the age of the painting. Those screws told me the painting had been tampered with. It also meant he had devalued the painting overall by replacing those screws. With that said it didn't matter to

Augustus if this painting was damaged or not because the painting inside this one would be worth so much more.

I used my knife to undo the screws as quickly as I could. It took longer than I wanted but it always did. Stealing art you had to have patience. It took time to get to what you wanted. There were security teams you had to worry about, removing screws with a knife was time consuming and your escape was always slower than you wanted it to be so it didn't draw attention.

I removed the last screw and opened the back of the painting. There it was a small piece of canvas with a young man looking back at me. I pulled the painting from the frame and replaced the screws as best I could. I checked the time, seeing that I still had two minutes. Placing the painting in my purse made me nervous as I began to roll the canvas. The canvas felt too fragile for my liking. I went with my second option. I pulled the K-tape and a small piece of thin cloth. I placed the painting face down on the cloth and added the other piece on top. I lifted my dress and secured the material to my body. I hung Love and Dread back on the wall gently and gave it one final look before I left. Jasper was leaning against the wall at the end. The guards' bodies were gone. I didn't ask what Jasper had done with them. I moved quickly down the hall.

"Did you find it?" Jasper asked.

"It was where I said it would be." I whispered.

I took his hand in mine and moved us down the hall.

"We have about thirty seconds before the loop stops." Jasper warned me.

"Then we better get back into place now."

We rounded the corner and resumed our positions. I looked up at Jasper and kissed him. I felt as the phone in his pocket vibrated. It was an alarm saying our time was up. Our kiss ended and I smiled at him.

"It's time to go, don't you think?" I suggested.

"Yes, I do."

Jasper took my hand as we made our escape. We moved through the people and reached the front door. I could feel his need to move at a faster pace.

"Keep your pace slow otherwise someone will notice." I warned Jasper.

Jasper slowed his movements down but I could feel the tension in his body. We reached the car and didn't hesitate as we climbed inside. Jasper drove us away from the Augustus' mansion, no one the wiser as to what had happened.

Chapter Sixteen

I called The Huntsman as Jasper drove us in the opposite direction.

"Do you have my painting, Red?"

"Why do you think I'm calling, Huntsman?" I answered sarcastically.

"There is no need to get snippy."

"Where do you want to meet?"

"Same place as we met before but on the top floor of the parking garage." The Huntsman replied.

"When?"

"In three hours."

"See you then."

I hung up and tossed the phone out the window.

"When and where?" Jasper asked me.

"The parking garage of the Hyatt, top floor, in three hours."

Jasper nodded his head. There was silence for a moment between us.

"Look, I know we agreed that once this was done you would go into hiding for a few months but what if we changed the plan."

I looked at my wolf.

"Jasper, you know The Huntsman will do everything he can to try and destroy both of us as soon as he realizes what I did. We do not have any other choice in this."

"Phoenix..."

"No. This is how we protect each other. If Icarus finds out you are a wolf and helped me steal from one of your clients, you lose everything. If anyone finds out who I am, I lose everything and go to prison. The only option we have is to stick to the plan."

"I don't care if they find out about me."

Jasper pulled over and turned to face me.

"Jasper..."

"I love you."

I was lost for words. I wanted to say I love you back or to say let's have a life together.

"You are better than me and as much as I could see a life with you, this is who I am. And you are the male who chases individuals like me, Jasper."

"No, it's what you have done for a living just as working for Icarus is what I have done. It's not who I am."

I stared at Jasper. I loved him but I only knew this life.

"What am I supposed to do, get a nine to five job? I have no identity as Phoenix or job history. I am a thief and that's all I have ever been."

"Do you love me?"

I was silent for a moment.

"Yes." I answered honestly.

"That is all that matters. We will figure it out but I do not want to lose you." Jasper leaned towards me and I couldn't help but kiss him. He kissed me back. I was crazy to even consider this. How could we have a life together? What were we going to do? I ended our kiss.

"Let's get The Huntsman and go from there." I replied.

Jasper turned away from me and drove us towards the meet up.

JASPER PARKED THE CAR on the floor below the top floor of the parking garage. The next task was to remove the painting from my body. The thing with K-Tape is it was perfect for sensitive skin and creating support for a joint but it stuck to the body for three days before it came off easily. Jasper began to work the edges of the tape pulling it back slowly until he had enough of it lifted where he could remove the stripe. It hurt as he pulled it from my skin but the pain only lasted for a few minutes. My body was red from the tape but it would fade away. I placed the painting gently in my lap taking in its simplicity. It was a painting that didn't have great details but it was done with care. It was a priceless painting that I wasn't in love with but the thought of giving it to Silas hurt.

Eventually, we began to chat as time moved slowly. Jasper was willing to walk away from his job in Icarus as long as I was willing to consider a different life as well. He wouldn't force me to walk away from being an art thief immediately but I would need to make a plan to start a new life as Phoenix Redmont. I sat and thought about what he was offering and asking of me. It was reasonable. We both wanted a life with one another. I liked the idea of starting over and not having to live several lives all at once. I would be allowed to just be me. It was something I hadn't done in years. I could sell several of my properties to create a cushion for myself while I began to build a new life. Or I could rent them out. I owned several properties across the United States. Renting them out would give me the income I would need to live off of. I could also sell the handful of pieces I had I didn't care about. That would make me a large amount of money that would help me in the long run. Jasper and I could keep one of my properties for our home and figure out what we wanted to do after that.

At the same time, it was also a scary prospect. I hadn't been Phoenix Redmont since I was a young adult. Could I do this? I would be starting from zero. I wasn't sure how to do it. If I couldn't, I would break us apart. I didn't want that either. If I didn't try I wasn't sure if I could live with myself either. I was willing to try, which told me I was willing to create a new life just to have him. Either way, I would have to go into hiding for several months until the coast was clear. Jasper and I could figure out our lives after that.

The closer it got to the time for our meeting, the less we talked. We eventually fell into silence until a car drove past where we were parked.

We watched as it rounded the corner and headed to the top floor. I took a breath, knowing it was The Huntsman. Jasper handed me his phone.

"Remember, you have two minutes and then I'm heading up." Jasper warned me.

"Jasper, maybe we should just hand it off to him and let him go with the painting."

"We have no idea what he will do with that or when. If we wait it will mean, we could lose the evidence we need."

Jasper was right but I didn't like it.

"Okay."

I gave him a quick kiss before I stepped out of the car. The painting in my left hand was loosely rolled up. I headed for the stairs, moving quickly. I opened the recording app and pressed the button before I reached the top. I slipped the phone into the top of my bra and took a few breaths.

There was only one car in the lot and it was The Huntsman's. His thin body was leaning against the car. His hands in his pockets and his ankles were crossed. He was so at ease which angered me. I approached him.

"It's good to see you, Red."

The Huntsman smiled cockily at me.

"Sorry, I can't say the same."

"You do look good all dressed up." Silas' eyes moved up and down my body. He stood up and walked towards me. "Tell me, where is your wolf?"

"What do you mean?" I questioned him.

"Do not be coy, Red. I know he is here." The Huntsman looked around for a moment.

"He's not here." I answered flatly.

His head dropped down low as he stared at me as if I was his prey.

"He returned to New York and then abruptly took time off. No one has heard from for the past week."

"I don't know where he is. I haven't seen him in a week. I did as you forced me to do. Do you want the painting or not?"

"Oh, I do, but not before you tell me where your wolf is." Silas closed the distance between us.

He placed a thin hand around my throat. He didn't squeeze but the threat was there. I pulled away from him.

"Do you think you scare me, Silas? You don't. Take your painting and go." I lifted my hand offering him the painting.

The Huntsman smiled crudely at me. I went to turn away from him but he grabbed my arm and pulled me against his body.

"You are beautiful but also a liar, Red." He locked his arm around my shoulders. He brushed the side of his face against mine. "You know where he is and I want him. Did you call your big bad wolf to help you? Is he hiding from me now?"

"We had a de..."

Silas pulled his face away from mine.

"Yes, we did, but then your wolf did a disappearing act and that changes things for both of us. I will ask you again where your wolf is and you will tell me. Or, I can take the painting and you with me as an insurance policy."

His words created panic in me. I hit him and began to push away from The Huntsman.

"The fuck you will." I said as I trie to get away from him.

The Huntsman smiled at me as he locked around me tighter.

"I'm right here, Silas." Jasper yelled as he moved silently over the concrete.

I made a move to step away from The Huntsman's grasp but not quick enough. His hand closed around my throat as he swung me around pulling me against his body. I held onto the painting as the two stared at one another.

"I knew you couldn't be far from her." I could hear the excitement in his voice. "She must have been a truly good fuck for you to put everything on the line, Jasper."

Jasper growled.

"Release her or I will fucking destroy you." Jasper threatened.

"Not before I kill her. It's your choice, Jasper. Killing me means she dies first.' Silas taunted.

"I have the painting. Do you want it or not?" I offered. "Just take it, Huntsman! Just take it and go!"

There was a pause as Silas turned his attention back to me.

"Raise it up slowly and let me see it." I did as I was ordered. I unrolled the painting and showed it to him. "Good job, Red. I have to say I am impressed with your abilities." I could feel his breath on me. I was trying to calm down as I stood still. "Now, I am going to release her and take what is mine. One wrong move and I will snap her pretty little neck."

The Huntsman released his hold on my throat slowly. I felt as his hand took the canvas from me. He pushed me away from him roughly. I hit the pavement hard and my right arm and leg scraped along the ground. I heard the snarl of my wolf as he launched himself at The Huntsman. Jasper's hands transformed from human to wolf as the two fought. His clawed hand closed around The Huntsman's throat. I watched as he gagged and struggled to breath. The painting was still clutched in his hands. I began to crawl towards the fight when Jasper's body bent back slightly as he howled in pain. He released his hold on The Huntsman, his hands going to his stomach. The Huntsman rolled Jasper off of him and stood up. The canvas still in his hand and a large buck knife in the other. I could see claw marks on his neck as he stared down the wolf. I could see as the blood dripped from the blade.

"NO!"

"I told you not to cross me, Red. Now, look at what you made me do." The Huntsman taunted me. I made a move towards Jasper. "Do not move, Red." He pointed his knife at me.

"I just want to help him." I held up my hands.

He smiled at me as I watched blood begin to hit the concrete from Jasper's body.

"You will not move until I leave."

"Huntsman..."

"Once I leave, you can help him. Otherwise, I will be forced to hurt him worse or maybe

even you."

Blood was pouring out of Jasper's body. I stood watching as The Huntsman backed away from us slowly. He climbed into his car and drove away. I waited long enough for him to get to the first ramp. I crawled to Jasper as his hands shifted back into human form. I knelt down next to him. The wound was more than a simple stab wound. The Huntsman had stabbed Jasper and then pulled the knife to the left, cutting not only tissue but organs as well. Blood was rushing from his body as I placed my hands on the wound trying to hold it closed.

"You have...have to...go."

"No," I cried. "You need to shift."

"I...I...can't. He must be..." Jasper's words fell.

"You have to try!" I demanded of him.

"Red...if the cops... find you with me, they will ask questions. I...I can't have that. Go."

"I'm not leaving you."

I held pressure over the wound, tears sliding down my face.

"You have to. Go...Now."

"I will not leave you. Not like this." I argued. "NOW FUCKING SHIFT!"

Jasper's body began to shake. I was confident that The Huntsman's knife had some form of poison on it. Between the severity of the wound and the poison, he was going into shock. I pulled the phone from my bra and tried to dial 9-1-1. I kept hitting the wrong buttons. I pulled my other hand from my wolf's body. I began to dial once more.

"9-1-1 what's your emergency?"

Before I could speak Jasper pulled the phone from my hand.

"I was...stabbed...I'm in the parking garage... of...The Hyatt Hotel...Help!" Jasper hung up the phone. "Please...go. I swear I will...find you."

"I can't leave you. Not yet."

I pressed my hands back over the wound causing Jasper to groan.

"If they...find...you here. Please Phoenix!" I shook my head, hating the idea of leaving him. He was my wolf, mine, and I was his. "Please!" I could hear sirens in the distance. I looked at Jasper who nodded his head. I leaned forward and kissed my wolf goodbye. "I will find you."

"I love you." I said around the tears.

I fled as fast as I could. The stairwell was my best option to not be seen. I still had my cap on which allowed me to cover my head. I kept my head down as I ran floor after floor. I heard the police and ambulance arrive in the parking garage as I reached the bottom floor. I waited inside the stairwell long enough for law enforcement to head to the top. I ran as fast as I could just as my wolf had said to do. I fled the scene as I made my way through the soundless streets of Savannah. I said a silent prayer to the fates asking for Jasper's to survive and a chance to burn Silas for what he had done to us. I now had a new mission in life: to destroy The Huntsman.

Don't miss out!

Visit the website below and you can sign up to receive emails whenever S.K. O'Brien publishes a new book. There's no charge and no obligation.

https://books2read.com/r/B-A-GGJY-HZDNE

BOOKS 2 READ

Connecting independent readers to independent writers.

About the Author

S.K. O'Brien is not just one person but two. Sammantha and Kyle O'Brien are the authors of The Daemon series and soon to come The Master Thief Series and The Queens. They are not only building a life with one another but also worlds inside of The Hellborn Series. They spend their days either writing as a team or laughing and enjoying life with one another and their kids.